THE MODERN LIBRARY TORCHBEARERS

BY ELAINE KRAF

I AM CLARENCE

I AM CLARENCE

A NOVEL

ELAINE KRAF

Introduction by Sarah Manguso

THE MODERN LIBRARY

NEW YORK

Published in the United States by The Modern Library,
an imprint of Random House, a division of
Penguin Random House LLC, 1745 Broadway,
New York, NY 10019

THE MODERN LIBRARY and the TORCHBEARER colophon are
registered trademarks of Penguin Random House LLC.

First published by Doubleday in 1969

Paperback ISBN 978-0-593-73185-7
Ebook ISBN 978-0-593-73184-0

Printed in the United States of America on acid-free paper

modernlibrary.com
randomhousebooks.com

1st Printing

FIRST EDITION

The authorized representative in the EU for product safety
and compliance is Penguin Random House Ireland,
Morrison Chambers, 32 Nassau Street, Dublin D02 YH68,
Ireland, https://eu-contact.penguin.ie.

To Jim

INTRODUCTION

SARAH MANGUSO

I Am Clarence, first published by Doubleday in 1969 when Elaine Kraf was thirty-three, is a fable-like, marvelously haunting depiction of an emotionally unstable, occasionally psychotic single mother's life. She narrates and evaluates the measure of her love for Clarence, her severely disabled and aphasic son, adding asides like "I smile and speak coherently reporting everything. (Everything?)" (page 6).

Kraf's novel asks us to consider the limits of maternal love and the components of a worthwhile life. Might such a life ever belong to a person with Clarence's physical and intellectual impairments, or to a person like his mother, whose every living hour is trained on his nurturing and survival at the expense of her own? How much should a mother be expected to sacrifice?

Mother and son's life together revolves around attempts to entertain, understand, and diagnose Clarence. His mother often brings him to the zoo, where "We do not go ... to learn. I do not assimilate new things quickly. Nor am I very curious. We just look" (page 136). At the circus, she dances and Clarence helps care for his beloved Josephine, the elephant. At the newspaper stand, Clarence's intellectually impaired friend Carl spends his days with his own beleaguered mother. Medical specialists try to make sense of Clarence's various disabilities; the boy's vision, mobility, digestion, and intellect are compromised, but the doctors remind us repeatedly that his hearing is perfect.

While she was pregnant with Clarence, his mother scheduled an abortion, but she changed her mind while on the operating table, moments before the doctor began the procedure. Her decision is presented as irrational, perhaps as proof of her mental unwellness, perhaps as a means of blaming her for her apparent predicament. She revisits it frequently, as if to make sure she made the right choice.

She harbors a vague paranoia that ebbs and flows. When she admits to perceiving things that no one else can see—scaring those around her—she willingly commits herself to an institution for many months, where, she says, "Patients as well as doctors observed my actions continuously. Sooner or later they would discover what I had done. The fear of discovery kept me in a constant state of anxiety. But occasionally it diminished" (page 69). One assumes that she feels guilty for almost having aborted her pregnancy; even so, the guilt seems outsized and vague. While his mother is thus encumbered, Clarence stays with his mother's brother, Elliot, and Elliot's wife, Sarah, who care for him lovingly. Their life together is conventional and calm, and one dares to wonder if Clarence might be better off with them.

Kraf also interrogates common assumptions about love and sex. The romantic dyad is presented as one of many possible arrangements within which people might find emotional, financial, and sexual safety and care. We watch various characters approve or disapprove of Clarence's mother with every decision she makes; we read editorial comments on her personal life from her brother, her sister-in-law, her psychiatrist, her neighbor, and others who take over the narrative for a chapter or two.

The book's warmest depiction of love, though, might be that of the relationship between Clarence and his friend Carl: "They discover every day that they can take turns looking through the pieces of cellophane they find on the street. Then they forget. But they do not forget for very long that being together is the important thing. Their tears and sounds stop quickly. Then they take hands and run somewhere." Their connection is authentic, unfettered, and rare in this fictional world of lonely and misunderstood people.

Formally, the plot proceeds skittishly, from multiple narrators who split their focus between internal and external foci. Many paragraphs contain what seem like a mishmash of unrelated sentences: some describe the parts of Clarence's eyes and the medical treatments thereof; some recount Clarence and his mother's games with felt letters or a tangerine; some speculate on which of the interchangeable men might provide a stable home for Clarence; some reveal how the mother feels she is performing as a mother, a woman, and a human being.

The narrative baton is passed among those who populate Clarence's life; hand-to-mouth artists and performers, medical specialists, and the assorted men who enter his mother's romantic orbit for days or years. Bits of sense data and dialogue hint at past events not depicted on the page; sometimes they are mentioned again later on, in a monologue by someone else. From the chapter entitled and narrated by "Any Man": "More goes on in that house than meets the eye. But I close my eyes. It is none of my business" (page 96). The novel comes into focus as a study of the negative space around a person possessed of almost no language. (The book's gnomic title does not appear in the text itself.)

The mother's intentionally amateurish poetry occasionally interrupts the narrative, reminding us that she keeps at least this much of her mind turned toward something other than Clarence. She says that she's always writing poetry, and describes it thus: "Many of my poems sound alike. The stones are small and metallic. And often they are frozen like stars" (pages 44–45).

Mysterious persons and objects appear and reappear, and initially one is not sure what is real and what is metaphor. Is there really a circus? Of what significance is the elephant? What of the singing waiter? What of the green ring, buried and dug up again? Many of the chapter titles alone perform feats of narrative potency: "Honey Standing on Sylvia's Shoulders Looking Into the Trailer," "Carl's Dream Before He Dies," "Ferdinand Under the Earth."

Everything is happening at once and yet there is no apparent progress; this is the state of being of the single, financially strapped mother of a profoundly disabled child. The mother's romantic life doesn't move beyond casual dating and a single rebuffed proposal; Clarence ages but does not mature; the rhythm of their days, though they occasionally move apartments and cities, remains consistent. But these grab-bag paragraphs are each a carefully arranged bouquet, positioned thus to suggest Clarence's experience of the world as a swirl of associative sensory input—and to ask whether that isn't the way we'd all be experiencing life if we weren't so intent on screening most things out.

Kraf maintains this uneasy ambiguity until the very end of the book, when its innermost secret is finally revealed, bringing a resolution that feels at once startling and inevitable. I'm still thinking about what more I should have noticed, how I might have anticipated the ending, how I could have done better, maybe stepped in—the story felt *that* real, a clear triumph for such an unnerving funhouse mirror of a novel.

—

SARAH MANGUSO is the author of nine books, including the novels *Liars* and *Very Cold People* and the nonfiction books *Ongoingness* and *The Two Kinds of Decay.* Her work has been supported by a Guggenheim Fellowship and the Rome Prize. She lives in Los Angeles.

I AM CLARENCE

CLARENCE AND I

It amazes me that Clarence and I have gone on so long. Always searching. Hand in hand, or he hopping zigzag behind me as I walk. My eyes are in the treetops. They live in the half dead leaves, or in an ancient rag tied to a bare twig, way at the top. There are also broken balloons—pink, red, who died inside out, squeezed at the neck, suddenly hissing.

Clarence hugs the thin trunks as we walk. Or he bends over in jerky movements to study a fly. It is a giant horsefly atop a mountain of stool. He cannot see very well (so they say, and I acquiesce), consequently his head gets too close. Puzzled, he lifts the fingers he has been leaning on. Forgetting to balance himself, he falls in some twisted position. (They told me, once, he wouldn't walk. He lay on his back for a long time like the lame elephant with one foot in the air; the withered limb beneath.) I untangle his legs. Bending, I wipe stool from his nose and from the thick lenses of his glasses; glasses refracting trees, endless sky, creases in my face. Lenses which insist, cover, assist, betray Clarence's eyes.

What he sees. Ophthalmologists are confused, suspicious, or certain. I listen to their speculations: peripheral cataracts, intra-ocular pressure, vascular abnormalities, exudates in the vitreous, cobble patterns on the retina.

And everything is the result of an unknown systemic disease, a bizarre internal malformation like midgets with shrunken wombs, or hands without fingers. Me—my chromosomes, my life in him. Does it matter? He used to laugh when the clowns came close to him, twisting their red mouths, or when the elephant swung him up high.

I listen to their speculations. I hear. I do not hear. My eyes are fixating branches as new lenses are ground; plus and minus fused together by optometric genius. Does it matter how precise the correction—he cannot say what he sees.

Is the physiological eye sufficient for their explanations? They know the eye. I know. Even I do not know what Clarence sees. Nor am I interested in the chaotic hieroglyphs of his brain waves.

(Dimension is lost, sometimes, even to me. Faces, walls, and windows are flat like cardboard deceptions.)

"His hearing is perfect," said the young intern. And I hung silver bells above his crib. That was long ago, not now. But sometimes I forget the sequence of events. The burglar gates were put up for our own protection, I believe.

Classified as "blind, for all practical purposes," I swear he sees the iridescent wing of an ordinary horsefly. Strangely, the fly remains stationary. Is it because Clarence's touch is as light as its own fibrous wing? Or are his insect legs hopelessly embedded in dung.

Down one thousand streets we walk, Clarence and I. Unconscious of time, I wear red, or orange, sometimes yellow. Because it is so hard to continue. I can sense when Clarence has ceased to follow. Automatically I stand still wherever I happen to be. By the time I move a second backward, he is marching forward again.

He touches my arm as I light a cigarette. Then he sniffs the smoke, laughs, and runs ahead. Gradually I catch up with him, and once more he is behind me. I am puffing smoke into the sky. He is examining a dirty newspaper, a leaf, a dead pigeon. He touches the sidewalk with his palm. (His friend Carl used to cry because the sidewalk burned. But Clarence likes the heat.)

What does it matter if he sees nothing, is mute, and falls writhing to the ground?

I smile as we enter the Diagnostic Clinic. A faceless lady accepts a jar of his first morning urine. Neatly I have typed: CLARENCE, FIRST MORNING URINE, and the date. In this I have improved, knowing the day, month, year, and finding directions easily. (In the institution I did not know names or dates. Now it has changed; I remember things most of the time, but I know I can forget.) There are things I cannot find or understand.

It is not the first time. We are always searching. Even if there are no answers in the end.

—

They take a part of him and study it. His blood smeared over one million slides, feces separated into constituent elements, enigmatic drops extracted from his glands. I watch. I have permitted it to happen; everything. (It could have been prevented, I think.)

Is there a magician to decipher each fragment and compound them?

His heart is perfect, but they insist. Taking a scribbled scroll from the electrocardiograph technician, we go upstairs. (They know us here. I do not even wonder what they think. I used to. Nor do I get headaches and take him home trembling.) He had wiggled his feet distorting the rhythm of the lines. But no one is concerned. Endless, limitless as things are, what is another distortion? For example, Ferdinand offered me a green ring. On certain days I am sure of it.

"Tangerine," says Clarence, surprising the diagnostician. Occasionally he does find a word if his want is precise—if he can, if the word is one of the few he has selected. (No one knows how. Even I.) "Tangerine" is one of Clarence's words. And he has kept it. He loses most of them; even his favorites. He lost "Mommy" a while ago. Maybe it was a few years. Not that it has any significance.

(I think of his delicate fingertips separating each section and then peeling off the peculiar whitish latticework. He likes to make it smooth, pulling this stringy substance from the fruit.)

His other words are: "bird," "feathers," "elephant," "hat," "Carl," and "Josephine." That is all.

I open my traveling bag and give him a tangerine. He rolls it along the floor. It stops between the swollen ankles of an elderly lady who is waiting in the Hypertension Clinic. She bends. Fascinated by the silken texture of her wrinkled hand enveloping the tangerine, he has forgotten. He places her hand against his cheek and closes his eyes.

"A seizure," says the diagnostician, looking back at Clarence, whose eyes are closed in ecstasy.

It goes on like that. He follows us from floor to floor, studying Clarence. Accompanied, sometimes, by a psychiatrist, speech pathologist, neurologist, or intern. "To leave no stone unturned," is the rationale. But what? Is there some conclusion that Clarence and I are waiting for. Why? Have I not created him as he is? I smile and speak coherently reporting everything. (Everything?)

—

After Clarence's skull has been X-rayed and more appointments have been made, we go through the hospital tunnel. It curves endlessly, tiled white, mysterious below the street. Nurses, doctors in white laugh, moving toward us. We glimpse fragments of their faces. (There is no green, no tree, but barren ground.) Men pass us, wheeling carts of filthy sheets, trays, cartons, unknown implements, prosthetic hooks.

A boy, covered with a sheet, stares at the harsh ceiling light. Then he disappears. Seated in wheelchairs, with sinister smiles, some are breathing with bottles of fluid going from chair extensions into their veins. (How has it come to this?)

It ends when we go into the coffee shop on level E behind Atran Laboratory.

Unexpectedly he begins to cry. If only I could understand. Is it Carl, or Ferdinand, or the lame elephant parading before him? I understand. Sometimes I think I do. Or is it only me?

I take out a tangerine and we roll it back and forth to each other over the cold table. Table spotted with tears. Time dead. Nothing but tangerine skin. I to him. Him to me. Fluorescent blue and distant clatter.

(It has happened like this before. Our solitude interrupted by a zookeeper, clown, derelict, madman, fool. Men; cardboard, flat, unknown. "Can I help?" The same thing. When Pierre found Clarence's hat, when Seymour took us to the beach. A hundred strangers have stopped at our tables. Has Clarence ever seen them. Not even I am certain. The year could be 1960, 1967, or tomorrow.)

I continue rolling the tangerine, not wanting to be anywhere else, or to answer. Who? He is taking apart blood, finding disorder in chromosomes. Night and day peering at the cells; erythrocytes, leukocytes, thrombocytes, he tabulates, scribbles, inventing new combinations, organizations of rings or chains. "I am a hematologist."

"He has had tests, and things are being questioned."

Inexplicably three of us are rolling the tangerine. (Each is the same.) His eyes invade everything. Soon he will win my confidence. The exact prescription of Clarence's present orthopedic shoes will be revealed. I will tell of the oddities of his growth, his unwillingness to associate objects with words. And his inability to learn as man is supposed to learn. Nor will the peculiarities of Clarence's eyes be forgotten.

I look at him, thinking I see a clown or violinist. When I am tired I cannot distinguish things. Hematologist, I tell myself.

He wants to know everything. I comply. We converse as he looks warmly, probingly, into the microscopic pupils of my eyes. I smile, a phantom. (I have never left the mirror where I saw his head come forth.) I never leave anything. It is all there, in circles, as I smile.

—

We are alone once more, Clarence and I, to our games and reveries. The sun dripping violent orange attracts Clarence. He affixes his bones to the window bars. We are lucky living up so high. The sun glitters on the tops of buildings. We see night, black with stars, between the crisscross of our burglar gate.

"Clarence is blind for all practical purposes," said the ophthalmologist. "He's a bit old, but we'll try occluding his better eye. Amblyopia ex anopsia."

When was that? He tears it off in a frenzy. (It doesn't look badly, though. Neither do his shoes.) He falls more often and has lost interest in the picture books. I threw away the patch last year. Maybe I did it yesterday or a long time ago. He kept falling and didn't enjoy the picture books. I should not have done it. But he became so quiet after Carl died.

Often it comes back to his eyes. But that isn't the main problem. If he could speak, maybe the sensitivity of his eyes would decrease. As it is, the slightest change in the atmosphere affects him. The conjunctiva reddens. A lump of blood appears in the bottom of his cornea. Pressure rises within. Occasionally the surface of his eye becomes very hard and he vomits and screams. Then drugs are given. But it isn't a typical case. In many instances they cannot find structural reasons for these changes. The iris-corneal angle, for example, is deep and perfect. (It wasn't always this way. It changes.) He loves to look at the sun, or into lamps. He turns the lamp on and off, pulling the copper chain all night.

This evening Clarence is weeping. His tears do not dry up. Nor are they accompanied by sobs. The veins of his thin neck pulsate as he stands bent backward for balance, knees apart, and toes pointing inward. His arms are outstretched, thin fingers spread apart. It is a grief without name, maybe never known before. Nor is it dependent upon concept. Chemistry is everything;

emerging from my own body whose warped chromosomes went on indifferently perpetuating.

Something about this day has caused his grief. Futureless, without space as it was in the clinic, under the lady's skirt touching her swollen ankles. Or covered with a black plate in the X-ray Department. Even I cannot know.

He used to be different. If a man came to the house and played with him on the rug he stopped crying. Now he does not run to the door or window. That was how it used to be, not how it is now, our heads in the tree, breathing, sightless. This excess is not good for him. Desiccation is inevitable. Pain will follow, then ulceration. (I have always known the dry, arid land and hated it.)

But is this a time to end.

We have gone on this long, come this far to the stone steps of the Diagnostic Clinic. (I used to remove the occluder when he cried. Or the brace when it squeezed his legs. But when? Didn't we ride the elephant? Sometimes we didn't even fall.)

"Clarence," I call. He turns his head, breathing with his mouth open. I bring green feathers, paste, sticks, and one of the distorting mirrors from Ferdinand. He pushes them away. (The same solutions cannot work. I know that.) Tomorrow I will buy him a parrot.

I give him his Dilantin, and we go out for a walk, wrapped in sweaters, wearing alligator boots. His tears are still coming. The street will divert him. I talk to him as I have always done except when I was in the institution; or the times I have trouble with sentences, constructions. (Words still slip away.) Ferdinand died; after the circus and all the elephants. Once he asked me to marry him. A green ring came to me from a midget who dug it up where he buried it. She kept it awhile.

———

We are not always by ourselves. We meet men often, as often as ever. At first they are kind. Then it diminishes. Is this why Clarence is crying? How can I tell him to accept the flow of things without despair. If I knew in what way he felt it most. (He used to stand at the door or window.) When, after bringing him rattles, mallets and plastic soldiers, they do not return—that must be it. Worse they lose interest. He brings his book of elephants and they look away. He keeps bringing it. Then he stops. He doesn't even play. He stays underneath the bed. He cannot understand. Why are things not the same, Mommy? Then I could try to answer. But even I wonder. Is it not preordained; the contrast between beginning and end being so extreme. Do they plan it. Or was there an initial pity, a fascination that they could not sustain. Clarence has not even the frail weapon of logic. What he sees he touches.

The telephone rings soon after we take off our sweaters. It is the hematologist, who cannot forget my eyes. Microscopic pupils seeing nothing... "Come over," I have always said, foreseeing the end. And the walk has not dried up his tears.

I wonder if it is not better for us to remain alone. (Who is coming today, I wonder, wringing my hands—but only for a moment.)

He arrives with a bouquet of carnations for me and nothing for Clarence. He looks at me. It is the same. We will go to bed if he wants to. It is simple. Clarence finally asleep and I in the hematologist's arms. Another night and Clarence in the morning—on the elephant, under the bed, dancing, falling... no end.

"I want so much for you," he says prematurely. I do not wonder. I know no more than he knows. Clarence, I say, he means something nice. I don't know why if it ends they say it at the beginning. Then something happens. Silence later; later no one banging at the door. Ferdinand dead. I don't want that. Clarence, don't cry. They mean something.

He stuck his finger into the center of the tangerine not noticing the hematologist, his gray moustache hairs bristling, seeming to advance, wanting to play with Clarence whose eyes are crushed together from crying; we bathe them in a warm solution. We always have. The man's hands are gentle. He is an actor or a man with tattoos or a hematologist. You. He likes being kind, for a moment. I see. Whistling, kissing me on my cheek or ear—when will it end?

I serve eggs flecked with parsley. Always. He eats hungrily, the egg sticking to his moustache or beard or teeth.

"Do you have a house for us? When?" I think or stop.

We drink coffee. Drops cling to his moustache. Clarence is indifferent. A few years ago he would have danced, receiving a broken violin from Seymour. But he does not. We know that nothing has changed.

He returns to his laboratory, below level E, after kissing me senselessly with averted eyes. (No trees, no air, only arid ground.) In a hurry, his wet moustache smelling of coffee and sleep. His breath reverberates, eggs, time. "Good-by."

He is not here now. Now or ever. (No one was ever here, were they?) The separation is complete like a scissor snip. Apart, seated with slides of blood, computing the possibilities for future generations of irregular genes.

Clarence, silent, not nodding or dancing sits with eyes pasted together unable to cry. He makes nothing out of it.

I have taught him to dress. He does it well, not caring what he pulls out of his drawer. Or caring too much. If it is a bad combination, I do not change it. Slowly his fingers are buttoning the purple shirt. (Their stares mean nothing.) He sits. I wish he was crying or wanting something. Don't die. It will be delayed—the laser beam that is going to seal the retinal fissure. I am glad it will not be today. We will rest; even for a whole year. Maybe there is something to do. Come out from under the bed. I will read a story about an elephant.

He will laugh not knowing, maybe knowing; what is the difference … if the chromosomes are degenerating or not, given to children and theirs. He is thinking, down there with fresh blood brought to the sub-basement in carts, about Clarence and me. We will not be thinking, or surprised if he has a toy or flowers.

Welcome, we give you all we have. That is the usual thing; bed, eggs, anything available at the moment. It is easier knowing that nothing has changed. Dates, philosophies, perhaps. Do you think philosophies change Clarence and me. They change our lives a little.

I wear red, orange, sometimes yellow, because it is hard to continue. We go out more often, to therapies and to the zoo. I attend social functions: The Society for Parents Without Mates, For Seeking Truth—others—leaving Clarence with a girl or old nurse. We have changed, you would say. I smile. Nothing has. Or they bring more presents, staying nicer longer.

—

When we are walking matter through matter, light of sun hitting us, warming, dazzling, blinding, I cannot turn back. We look at people coming toward us or walking alongside sprouting different things, being different ages, pursued, wanted, unwanted by degrees. And all this changing. His hand is wet in the center and the fingers are limp. Or they cut into my skin and I cry out. It is the day, the weather, or what he feels. (I have canceled the appointment with the ophthalmologic surgeon.) It isn't so bad living up here, the sun coming into the kitchen on the used plates. We go away and return. We play games and sleep.

A humpbacked midget, Alexander, ran away from the circus for no reason. We never knew him. No one heard anything. It is like us.

Where we walk, where we sit in silence. We like the luncheonette on Sixty-fifth Street; clockless, rugged, with white wrought-iron chairs. It doesn't matter how long it takes us. The waiters are polite in mustard-colored jackets with red lapels. We are handed menus like everyone. People live in the building above, in combinations we know nothing about. They wonder politely, seeing us there day after day. But we live far away.

We used to live in an apartment that had an entrance from the street. It was our own door across from a newspaper stand. She saw us going in and out; the newspaper woman. I don't know why she didn't like me. Now it is a bicycle shop. I don't like to pass it, seeing the sign BICYCLES, and how things change. (Clarence was attending a school for aphasic children then, hoping for speech. He has attended many schools. But he wasn't doing well. He wasn't improving they told me. And I could see that they did not want him there. Somewhere else, sometime, not when we lived there, they tried to teach him Braille with raised dots on big cubes. The teacher was patient, smiling. But any language is the same. We fail. [It didn't work.] And he had more seizures with all those children digging holes in paper clipped to slates or typing on Braille typewriters.) Any language is the same. I don't bother with it now. Maybe after the diagnosis is completed something can be attempted. I don't know what. Yet it seems better this way; here in the luncheonette without clocks, just listening to voices. (His ears are perfect.) The people come down from their apartments for lunch. It is just a circle perhaps. We are back to sounds. (He hears.) I am cautioned to guard against this. But they know nothing. And Ferdinand died of something cancerous. We are happy with sun on the smooth table. The people have mysterious things to do. They come and go in various costumes, changing a little each day. Some days they look quite unlike themselves. I am not sure who they are. We like it here. We are not rushed.

I will not be surprised if he calls later and brings flowers. Maybe he won't. I'm hoping that Clarence's eyes will get better today. They have begun to open slightly. He breaks a glass, pounds on the table, and makes a shrill sound. Then he laughs. I sigh with joy. It is all right. Rugs muffle these noises. People hardly care. I am so glad. He is shaking the salt into a pile on the table. He makes many hills like the homes of ants.

—

Sometimes it gets like it is today; a mass of silence. And we are secluded inside it. Things are distant, not even menacing. Sentences come with difficulty. I am aware that it is a kind of regression. I am resting. If I really wanted to, I could stop it, come closer to things again. If I wasn't so tired. I am sorry. I don't care to do anything but what we are doing, sitting here. Later, if he brings them, it will be night. That will be for someone. It is pleasant to go to sleep with someone; not changing anything at all. I know. I realize. Even if his answers to the questions were right. "I have a house for Clarence." There would still be so much—explanations about origins. Where I was, what I did the other years. (I am not sure now. Sometimes I am.) I know about that. If they successfully suture his retina with the laser beam and secure it to the scleral globe, that will be something. Once they cut into his scalp. I let them do that. It helped, in a way. Otherwise I am not certain. Perhaps it will be next week. They have insisted that I have a plan of some kind. I try. I cannot structure the hours. Is that best anyway? Why is this not enough. We go over the felt letters. He touches them and I say them. I say, give me a C. Sometimes he does. Or he forgets and gives me an M instead. He prefers O to any letter except X. Is it important that it is not a C. It is also a game. We play it every single evening except when I am tired.

(I think I have gone on like this long enough, sometimes.)

———

They pressed his head face down against the black table. His nose was pushed into it. The plate pulled from inside said CLARENCE on it. Buzz. "Hold your breath." He didn't know. But the plate had his bones.

Their eyes look after us as we walk away from these tables— yellow, stippled, pebbled, white, or black. In the zoo or outside. He skips and falls. I walk in the same way, revealing nothing. It happens over and over again, whether his pupils are dilated and I bring tinted glasses to keep out the glare, or constricted with tiny prickles of light. We go home when it is over.

(Is my home the land of freaks where there is no green?)

After the crusts had been wiped away, the hematologist came serenely, gray-moustached, out of his laboratory with gladiolas. As if nothing had happened. I put them into the same transparent vase that I have always used always intending to get something blue. But it is the same vase whose dead leaves stink at the bottom.

—

Each day, then, is another story. And the same thing; zoo, aquarium, peanuts, pigeons, balloons, Egyptian mummies, or seals. His retina can always be re-attached if that is the problem, or certitude. Like the time the scalpel pierced his skull. (I did everything.) Something might, in fact, be done before Christmas. And that is coming soon enough, each year.

He whispers, "I like being with you everywhere." Like the actor who committed suicide or someone else. I acknowledge this, smiling, offering whatever I can. It doesn't matter if the year is gone or tomorrow. I search the Frigidaire and pull out an old fat chicken, sprinkling it with parsley flakes and thyme. "The day will come," he promises. I do not understand. I kiss him as though he has made up a poem or brought gladiolas. Sometimes he stares at Clarence with suspicion or scrutiny beneath his kind eyes. Or he plays with him listlessly on the rug. Clarence would prefer to sit in the luncheonette on Sixty-fifth Street where it is quiet. (But it is closed for renovation.)

If the elephant came back, it might be different.

After waiting in the corridor, wearing a long white gown, he was called inside. On the black table he breathed and drew circles in his breath's vapor. But he had to lie on his stomach with his cheek touching the cold surface. Why? Buzz. His eyes stared into voids. He knows nothing about it. I know. Buzz. CLARENCE, his name, engraved on the plate beneath his skull.

(Your life has nothing to do with mine...)

The man helped, bathing his crusted eyes. They began to

open. From heat the flowers spread out quickly. Desiccation was arrested. But they crumpled the next day. I discovered tiny vagrant bugs within, who had invaded earlier.

He had a friend once. That was when we lived where the bicycles are sold. I planted seeds in a window box, and they bloomed in wild profusion without care. Across the street the woman who sold newspapers watched her quiet mongoloid boy. He didn't see well either. And he often caught colds. I remember his watering eyes, tender white skin, the blue veins beating under his eyelids.

Days they sat together on a wooden crate, unbothered—laughing, fingering, peeling sticks, or squinting, finding glistening things below the curbstone. An ordinary leaf fascinated them for hours. Or the melting tar that stuck to the soles of their feet.

I watched, smiling, behind the flowers which hid my face, as their love grew and their hands sang with joy. It seemed like a beginning; green, fertile, new. (I almost wrote poems again.) It seemed so long but ended like a dream. Carl died and Clarence lay mute, without looking. Or if I took him outside he ran to search inside her newsstand, not understanding. How can he ever understand?

We moved away from the flowers and we have continued. As long as things continue, everything is all right. Let him laugh, make noise. Let a few flowers grow once more.

(When the limousine rounded the bend and I knew I still had the baby, I laughed with happiness... "I have him," I said. The instrument was ice cold that tried to open me and remove him, unformed... but I had him. I am so glad.)

———

We are happier up here than we ever were before. The windows look over the top of the city. We see the buildings turning gold, and we have dinner there, watching it get dark between the burglar bars.

Men come; many men; just as many as ever. But they should

have come when we lived in the apartment across from the newsstand. Clarence was happier then. I was prettier. And we had not been over so many paths, nor had there been all those deaths.

We were lonely. But everybody came. I know it. I can count them. I can wander back and forth remembering. Why does it seem as if we are always waiting? Is it true that everyone went away. Or that you rode a tame elephant without falling.

Aren't we happy, living up here, tracing letters, watching the sun? I cannot find the truth, sometimes, Clarence.

THE BIRTH OF CLARENCE

A masked man was sitting at the foot of the delivery table; I did not know who it was. (He wound the sphygmomanometer cuff tightly…a stethoscope was placed over the brachial artery and the valve slowly released…ss…sss…sss.) "Blood pressure is normal," said the nurse.

Masks hung everywhere: Trilene Masks, Oxygen Masks, Plexiglass, Cloth, Rubber, Tin, Plastic—they multiplied. I glanced away from them into the circular mirror. Why was it so far away—small, dusty, cracked.

"Record the foetal heartbeat," ordered the obstetrician. Something cold was placed low on my belly. "Normal," she said. I stared into it, above and far away. There was my own face, distorted, mutilated by the mirror's cracks.

"Oxygen," he said. Strange hands with shiny black gloves pushed a transparent mask in front of my face. I saw it in the mirror, and pushed it away. How could I be certain who…

The cervix dilated suddenly. I breathed quickly—puff, puff, puff—and then rested.

"Pethidine—one hundred milligrams," said the obstetrician. She prepared the syringe. "I have no pain," I said, refusing. Again the cervix dilated and I breathed faster—puff, puff, puff, puff, puff—and then rested.

"Wipe the mirror, and take away the masks," I gasped, as the contraction slowly subsided. (They looked at each other.) The masked man—an imaginary father, a dummy, imposter—stood up on a chair and wiped the mirror with gauze. He spit on it and wiped it again. (I smiled.)

Tic-Tic-Space—the next contraction came. Soon, soon, I thought. A hand wiped my forehead with a cold sponge. Then the obstetrician whispered something to the anesthesiologist. It irritated her and she muttered back rudely, glaring at him with hate. But she covered the masks with white cloths. They were less menacing but I knew they were there, waiting. I could see their outlines.

"No masks," I said, fully conscious, before a violent contraction pulled me open. I jumped into it gladly, too excited to remember to breathe from my rib cage. I lost count. (Nothing, nothing, nothing; I want to see. I want to be present, like the nights when I sang with the singing waiter under the stars; beneath my own roof. Do not diminish me with chemicals or false sleep. I am afraid of sleep.)

"Good," said the man who had cleaned the mirror. It was Ferdinand, the tattooed man, my lover; one of the false fathers. I felt better seeing him unmasked. He was pale, looking inside me for something. "Where are Franz and Albert, the clowns?" I asked before the next expansion began. There was hardly any time to rest now. Up, up I went with it, enjoying it, panting, puffing; not the way I had been taught—there were too many things on my mind. It didn't matter. Pain is proof.

There was a huge clock in the room. I imagined the clowns and midgets running round and round over the numbers, smiling. And from far away, the singing waiter sang a song about the moon. (I am lonely.)

"The head has descended to the pelvic floor," said the obstetrician. The nurse put the cold thing on my belly and recorded the foetal heartbeat. (Bum-ba…bum-ba…bum-ba…bum-ba…)

I held back, feeling it large. I held. "Push," ordered Ferdinand or the obstetrician. I had forgotten, concentrating on the mirror, wanting it so badly. "You're doing fine," he said in an unfriendly voice. (He wound the sphygmomanometer cuff tightly...a stethoscope was placed over the brachial artery and the valve slowly released...sss...sss...sss.) "Blood pressure is normal."

He was glaring at me, angry because I had forgotten to push. Then he whispered something. The anesthesiologist was tiptoeing behind me, reaching beneath a cloth to get the transparent plexiglass mask.

"No," I screamed. "Just this once, let us all be unmasked." They obliged, thinking it was the intensity of the contractions.

"All of them—firemen's masks, witch masks, Halloween masks, ape masks, and the paper masks from grade school." (They had terrified and intoxicated me at once.)

"You're doing fine," someone said.

Ferdinand, watching the rapid dilation of my cervix, lowered the mirror. (Thank you.) I saw something black and fuzzy inside. Mine, I thought, therefore I exist—if they let me. Please.

"Are you sure you don't want anything to take the edge off— just a small injection of chloral hydrate, sixty grams to make you drowsy." "Basal narcosis," echoed the nurse, absently recalling something from afar.

"No," I said. (I had to have absolute proof.) Time, contractions, vague thoughts of who I was, and the proof that I was myself—it was within me, struggling to emerge. Happy clowns and freaks danced before me. Elephants paraded, monkeys jumped.

I was about to... "Don't push yet," warned the obstetrician. (He was turning something around, facing another way. I saw him do it between my legs in the mirror. "Don't push yet," repeated Ferdinand, unmasked, watching me. I wished his chest was bare so I could see the blue snakes, green-blue dragon, and tropical birds.

That was me, wide open, and he was turning the other head around. I saw it.)

"Now!" And I let go and pushed through the mirror. I saw his head covered with hair—eyes, nose, mouth all wet—body coming out. His face was covered with hair. First one shoulder was pulled out and then the other. Arms followed easily. Out he slid, fastened to me. (I laughed out loud—he and me.) The mirror was cloudy. I didn't need it. I saw him, lifting my head, with his long, twisted body and misshapen skull, covered with hair and yellowish mucous.

The nurse stifled a gasp. She put an instrument into his nostril, extracting something like viscid slime so he could breathe. He made a choking sound and she extracted the same thick substance from his throat. Now he cried and now he breathed.

"Don't cut it," I yelled. Six inches down the cord was clamped. A ligature was wound around it. "Don't." But they did it, clipping him away. And a little later I pushed out the rest of it. It slithered out, emptying me completely.

I wanted to hold my twisted, hairy child; a boy. Briefly they laid him down on me. Then I slept.

THE SINGING WAITER

The singing waiter serenaded me. Elegant, in his red and white striped shirt with satin vest, he sang. From the candlelight his eyes were moist and tender. His basso was extravagant as he extended his arms, gazing at me with longing.

It was my twenty-ninth birthday, and Elliot and his wife had insisted upon taking me out to celebrate. I had accepted without enthusiasm.

He had disappeared, weaving gracefully between the tables when a note was presented to me. "May I join you? Your singing waiter, Joe Paliacco."

I scribbled my answer quickly. Soon Joe was striding forth, smiling and confident, making the room burst with mellow joy. He ordered a bottle of champagne, and I drank with tiny bubbles dancing in my brain.

When we left, the singing waiter returned to his work. He had said good-by and bent to kiss my hand.

Lying in bed that night the stars bit my lips and the entire Atlantic held me in its arms.

The next day he arrived wearing an old velvet hat and a long coat with a frayed velvet collar. His skin had a bluish cast, and his eyes were half-closed.

"Happy birthday," he said, smiling. And I recognized him in spite of his disguise.

I put the one blood-colored rose he brought in a jar of water. Then we left to see a Sunday afternoon performance of *Winterset*.

The moment we were seated, he excused himself, leaving his coat on the back of his chair. (I held the velvet hat on my lap.)

When he next appeared he was firing a gun from a dark alley under the Brooklyn Bridge. His collar hid most of his face; only his eyes betrayed a criminal's stare. For a moment I was not certain. He spoke his five lines well. Amazed, I wondered what had become of my waiter with his tender eyes.

Later he read *Othello*, with great fury, from a volume of *The Collected Works of William Shakespeare*. Cheap paper lanterns hung from the ceiling, and we sat amidst grand clutter, drinking wine.

His apartment was a small, roach-infested valise on Essex Street. Everything was strewn about and tumbling from dark corners; mutilated playscripts with pages missing, yellow photographs of dead actors, helmets, boots, miniature stage sets and posters. There were a few carefully framed photographs of himself as he appeared in summer productions. In one he was the mad Caligula, in another a moustached seducer, in a third the grinning Iago.

As he created himself, an endless stream of false persons, so he created me. I became the fragile Laura, beautiful Desdemona, ageless Helen, and Hamlet's tormented mother.

We played and drank, seldom touching the earth until Monday night. Putting on a freshly laundered red and white striped shirt, he became the singing waiter.

Depositing me at my door, he kissed my cheek and wished me a happy birthday once again. Then he was gone.

Night after night I waited for his call. I didn't care in what disguise he would appear. I needed his magic. I longed to journey again away from my world.

But the bloody rose had wilted and fallen away, leaving only its essential but useless pistil on a broken stem.

———

Two weeks later he appeared with a bouquet of wildflowers. We rode the ferry around Manhattan Island until late afternoon. Everything interested him, and so he fled (and I followed), from one end of the city to the other. We ate in hidden basement restaurants, where he was welcomed as a king. We explored barren beaches, looking for peculiar bulbous weeds, or gigantic spiral shells. Together, we tasted every kind of cheese, and saw unknown plays given in musty lofts.

He heightened the smallest thing; his eyes touched an ordinary pigeon, and it became a tropical bird with flaming pink and coral feathers hidden beneath its wings. (Hands empty, outstretched, I took the world he offered. Together we devoured everything. Alone nothing spoke, and I gave no response.)

Whenever Joe wanted to run, I was ready. And when he left, I dreamed of him. (Open my eyes. Give me the world.)

I knew Joe over a year before Clarence was born. He wore a moustache. He grew a beard. He shaved it and was dressed like a businessman. He wore a black leather jacket and rode a motorcycle. He drove a truck, a cab. He bought a cheap car. He walked. He worked. He borrowed.

Joe was always changing. I caught a glimpse of him and then he was gone. He returned in a new disguise.

I loved him passionately. Had he wanted me, I would have lived in his apartment on Essex Street—but it was his. Others came. I knew. I saw their stockings under the bed, or found a dress in the closet. I closed my eyes.

Nothing about Joe was consistent. He was impotent some nights, and passionate others, or wanting something even he could not imagine.

He called me every day, or forgot me for weeks. I'd be awakened in the middle of the night by a Western Union telegram of love, or left abruptly at some party. He often disappeared with someone else when we went out together. And I went home alone.

I always forgave him. I thought I did. What choice was there? I clung to him for my life.

THE LIMOUSINE

_____

(_Told by Elliot_)

I was watching television when she came in. I had been hoping
to get a phone call saying she had changed her mind and was
going to keep the baby. I don't think that babies who are partly
there should be taken out. That's just my opinion. It doesn't seem
fair. And I thought she looked happy since she found out. That
puzzled me. She never seemed so happy. My wife said pregnancy does that. It's the hormones, and it has nothing to do with
the decision. I didn't say, "How do you know, since you've never
been pregnant?" She can't. I guess she heard it from other pregnant ladies. My wife said it's the hormones that make her calm
enough to decide to let someone cut it out. "That means it's all
mixed up, and that she doesn't know what she's doing," I said.
My wife doesn't like it when I use the words "mixed up." That is
because so many things _do_ mix me up. So even when I use it another way she doesn't like it. Sometimes she says, "Elliot, why
does everything mix you up?" She means things like numerical
facts: percentages, or pints, quarts, and centimeters. Mostly she
means contradictions in people. I often don't understand the significance of the things that worry them. I am not lying. I don't
understand the things that people do. My sister always wanted to
have a baby, and now she was deciding to have it taken out. "I
don't know who the father is," she told us. We didn't care and
said so. But she said it wouldn't be fair to the baby. You could

read that any place. She'd picked it up; maybe in some magazine. And I don't believe that she felt that way. But my wife did. She thought it was reasonable. "You love babies," I said to her. I said it another day. I'm not so tactless as to have said it the day she was going to do it. "That isn't the point," she had answered.

When she came in, I was watching one of my favorite "soap operas." I don't hide it. I think they are very good, and many things about people can be learned from them. I don't like turning one off in the middle, but I did—the minute she came in.

We know each other, being brother and sister for so long. "There's no hurry," she said, looking that same calm way. "Let's finish watching the program." I turned it back on, and we watched it like normal people. It had only ten minutes to go. I remember it well because of that day: A nurse's husband had cancer and was staying in the same hospital where she was working. She liked to drop in on him, kissing him and saying nice things. She hid her fear. She knew but he didn't know what he had. He was beginning to get suspicious about why they were taking so long about letting him go home. "It's just routine," she said, smiling and urging him to take a pill to make him sleep. She kissed him good night and softly closed the door. Outside his room she fell apart, crying in the arms of an older nurse who was the head nurse. Then it faded out until next time. I turned it off. I watch it every day. My wife likes to work in the drugstore at the cash register. And I cook for her and make her comfortable. I don't like to go out of the house. It isn't a fear or anything. I just like it better inside.

My sister was lying on the couch with her suitcase near her. She had brought some things so she could stay overnight. She was dressed in an orange dress like it was a celebration of some kind. She had even put on lipstick and mascara.

A taxi was scheduled to arrive at 2:00. My wife drives, but she had to work. I know she would have taken the day off if she thought it was best. But she sensed that we wanted to go alone.

Seymour, who didn't know if the child was his or not, begged to go along. However, he had not begged her to keep the child. Nor had the other probable fathers, as far as I knew. I don't anger very easily, but that angered me, especially Seymour wanting to come along when it was being cut out of her. If my wife was pregnant, for example (assuming she was able to be), and she had a lover, four lovers, even seven, I would say, "Look, I want the baby. I am your husband and I will be father to your baby." Even if I wasn't married to her I would feel that way. I know that most men don't feel like this and wouldn't understand it. Even my wife who won't adopt a baby because it isn't from her body wouldn't like it. It is so clear and simple. Sometimes I think that people like to confuse things. That is why they don't see anything. They make everything very complicated. (Of course some people are more complicated than others. I am not a very complicated man.) In the "soap operas," people are a little more direct in their emotions, if nothing else. They seem to know what they want even if they can't get it. I don't see why a man should mind if the sperm from some other man made a baby. The baby is still nice. I guess it's a kind of possessive pride I never had about my specific sperm. I don't want my wife to sleep with another man; not unless she wants to very badly. I wouldn't love her less because she had had someone else's penis in her.

If you love a woman, you want her and her baby. That's all there is to it. Unfortunately no one loved my sister that way. I thought Seymour did. He used to be around her bringing flowers and boxes of chocolates and things. But he just wanted to come along. He had found a man he said was "competent." "She will have a dilation and curettage," Seymour had explained to my wife. Later, my wife explained it, and reminded me that she had had one for a cyst about four years ago. (It was true.) I had asked around, calling different doctors, but not telling who it was. I think maybe they recognized my voice. I said I was Mr. Hall. It didn't sound like a real name, particularly the way I said it, but that didn't matter. Most of them got scared at first and didn't want to talk. That is because of its illegality. But when I assured them that I only wanted information, and not for them to do anything, then they answered. But they were still anxious for me to get off the telephone. "Any other method," said one clipped voice, "and the woman is taking her life into her own hands. Even a curettage done outside a hospital without sanitary precautions can be dangerous." "There are some risks," said another, "depending upon the age and health of the woman."

When Seymour had driven her outside the city to meet the doctor, she came back upset. "I hate his hands," she had said. She had decided against it when she saw his hands. Then she changed her mind. I am not sure why.

———

What we thought would be an ordinary taxi turned out to be a limousine. It looked like a long black hearse. We got into it, sinking deep into its sponginess. Everywhere was space lined with soft cloth, padded with mute sponge. Leaning back, we rode past the congestion of the city, through smaller towns or suburbs where the air was fresh and the sun gleamed with clarity. My sister sang. I looked at her with disbelief. But I tried to think about those hormones. Her breasts were already huge, and almost instinctively she took excellent care of herself and drank large amounts of milk. To a man it was incredible. Her personality had changed. She admitted feeling well and calm—even today. "Don't worry, Elliot, I can accept what is going to happen. When it is finished I will rest. Maybe I'll go away. Then life will begin again." It sounded false to me. "But what will you feel when these hormones desert you." I wanted to say, "a sudden jolt, a falling." I knew my sister. If there was anyone I knew at all, it was my sister. This carefree attitude wasn't her. Either she was mad or full of hormones.

"Let's try to enjoy the ride, Elliot," she said. She knows me too. The driver, behind his glass partition, heard nothing. I don't know what he thought. We didn't look like people who ride in limousines out into the country. I prayed that the car would break down. And I am not a religious man. I hoped that the doctor would have vanished, and not until the last moment did I stop wishing for my sister to suddenly decide to turn back. But instead, she said, "Let's get something to eat. The doctor said I should eat something bloody before and after." We stopped at a diner, conspicuously getting out of the black hearse. The workers turned their heads in amazement. The driver remained looking at his hands behind the glass partition.

We both had roast beef sandwiches, and she had a glass of milk. My sister hated milk. I felt sorry for her. Evidently a part of her, at this very moment, was caring for and nourishing a baby she had decided to let float away. I patted her shoulder. "How do you feel?" I asked. "Sleepy but calm." "That's fine," I said. We entered the limousine a second time and were silent until the journey ended. He waited for us on a designated street. The doctor had requested that our car wait near, but not in front of his office.

—

His office was inside a pleasant ranch house not far from a lake. He was evidently quite a gamesman. Inside were the stuffed heads of bald eagles, deer, tigers, and even a rhinoceros. We waited under a bull's head for about an hour. The office was decorated with pots of yellow flowers, lithographs of tigers, and a tropical floor plant. The couch we sat on was brown tweed. There were armchairs of the same tweed, and some straight-backed, bare wooden ones. Only two patients had come before us. I will never forget them. One was a well-to-do lady of about fifty-seven, wearing a "good" gray suit. Her hair was stiff and tinted a horrible bluish-gray. She had a navy handbag and matching navy shoes with silver buckles at their centers. Bulging out of the shoes were the most swollen ankles I had ever seen. It was hard not to keep staring at them. The other was an adolescent boy. He had a childish face and a long body. He kept swinging his legs and cracking his knuckles. All the time he was staring at my sister's legs. It made me angry because of the situation. But she didn't even look pregnant unless you knew something about things like that. She looked prettier than she had looked before she was pregnant.

—

We had leafed through all the *Field & Stream* magazines when the two patients left, apparently in better spirits than when they had been sitting in the waiting room. Then the receptionist left, and we were alone. About fifteen minutes after she left, the doctor came out. "Come in," he said to my sister. She no longer looked so calm. But she followed.

I waited what seemed like hours. I leafed, paced, or sat and thought. I thought of the doctor's face. It was hard to tell much from that. He hadn't looked very kind, nor had he looked sinister. He probably took the risks so he could go on more hunting expeditions in Africa, or wherever they were. That must cost quite a bit with all the equipment and loss of working days. I tried to imagine what it would be like in Africa, and whether my wife and I would like to go there after she retired. Of course, we wouldn't do any hunting or go out to the wild regions except in a tourist's bus with someone who knew the animals and the terrain. People thought it was sad to die without having seen the whole world. My wife thought so. I didn't. I'm just not that curious. And I hardly ever feel deprived of things. I like my house and my wife. If I thought she minded my staying home, I would get some kind of job. But she doesn't mind. It worries me sometimes.

I tried not to think too carefully about what the doctor was doing to my sister. I expected to hear screaming. It was so quiet. That worried me too. Thoughts of blood and dead, half-made babies came into my head no matter how I tried to keep my eyes on the lithographs of stalking tigers. I thought of her as a little girl and tried to figure out how she came to be so unusual in her thinking and in the people she liked. But those things are mysteries. I wasn't really that interested. It was hard to wait out there in the silence, not knowing what was happening, or if you should go inside and stop everything, or just sit there quietly. I felt sick to my stomach.

She came out suddenly, pale and stumbling, walking with difficulty like it hurt between her legs. I almost threw up when I saw her. The doctor never showed his face. He hadn't even helped her out of the room. I led her, leaning on me, to the street where we left the black limousine. For the first time, the driver looked up with unconcealed interest. He knew that something peculiar was going on. But he didn't speak or roll up the glass that separated him from us. Maybe that was a rule given to drivers of limousines.

Once inside the car she passed out. I was frightened and thought about telling the driver to hurry. But I didn't want to knock on his glass partition. It didn't seem right.

He rounded a sharp bend and that woke her up. I sighed with relief. "I'm hungry," she said. "Elliot" (and then a long silence) "he almost took it out, but I changed my mind. He got very angry. The silver thing was cold. It had already opened me up so he could reach it. He had a hard time. That's why he was angry even though I had given him the money before." She was quiet for a while. I knocked on the partition. It rolled open. I asked the driver to stop in front of a grocery store. There, in some obscure New York suburb, I hopped out and bought her a hamburger and a few chocolate bars. My sister loves chocolate, even though she tries not to eat too much of it.

"I have the baby," she said. "He was about to start cutting it out, then I knew I wanted it. I said, 'No, no, stop.' He didn't want to stop. 'You're a fool,' he said, 'to come this far and then change your mind. And it's such an easy one.' But he stopped."

She smiled and ate the chocolate bars, but not the hamburger. She ate them and then she slept. She slept at our house for almost two days, waking occasionally and muttering, "I have him."

THE BIRTHDAY PARTY

He grew in his own way; I danced. Sometimes the night was black, and I walked blindly. Or I saw a star. Above his crib I hung a silver ball filled with bells. When the wind blew it jingled. He liked that. (His hearing is perfect.)

People came to see him, but only a few would touch him. The hair had not fallen off his body, and he made few movements. Nor did his eyes follow light unless it was very bright. The doctor said that his hearing was perfect. But he didn't know if Clarence would walk or what was wrong with his brain.

I heard only the good things, singing, laughing as I held him close to me. (I wrote many poems then about stars, dead leaves, and shining stones.)

Because there were many emergencies, we moved across the street from a hospital. Late at night he would choke, turning green. (I wrapped him in blankets and hurried to the Emergency Waiting Room.) Or he had violent convulsions, fits, and high fevers. Yet he survived, and his heart beat strongly. I listened to it with my ear against his chest.

His eyes were not good but he saw light and shapes. And I am certain that he recognized different people.

I waited for the words; there were hardly any sounds, just a lot of gasping and occasional crying. My brother Elliot and his wife were waiting for sounds and words. "Mama," they said, bending over his crib. But nothing happened.

The hair fell off his body in his fifteenth month; not that I minded it. It was the others who rejoiced. It fell off his head too, except for a small patch in the front, and never grew back.

When he was a year old, I gave him a birthday party. I invited Ferdinand, the tattooed man I had met two years before Clarence was born. He brought Franz and Albert, the clowns; a humpbacked midget, Alexander, who disappeared several months later; and a man eight feet tall. My brother Elliot and his wife, Sarah, came, but they felt strange among the freaks. Dr. Fishbain, a young intern who had helped us through many nocturnal emergencies, arrived with his wife Rena. She was a flat-chested girl with greenish-blond hair and watery eyes.

Clarence sat hairy and limp—a king receiving presents—from his red highchair. (He was propped up with many cushions and straps.) The presents were magnificent. Ferdinand brought a pink balloon which he shook near Clarence's ear, causing the pebbles to vibrate inside. He also brought the first of many distorting mirrors with which I later lined Clarence's room. Franz and Albert, dressed in clown white with polka-dotted suits, gave Clarence their pointed hats. Thus began Clarence's hat collection, one of his greatest and most lasting joys. (He laughed when they came up close, twisting their red lips.)

The tall man gave him a tambourine decorated with red ribbons.

As we sang "Happy Birthday to You," Clarence banged the tambourine and dropped it on the floor like any other child. And he smelled the many-layered birthday cake that Elliot had baked. When there was noise his body became less limp, and he moved his arm and one leg.

(Alexander, the humpbacked midget, sat in the corner, looking at the floor.)

When I think back to this first birthday, it seems a colorful and joyous event. But there were no other children there, and Ferdinand was the only one of Clarence's fathers that I invited. I regretted inviting Elliot's wife. I could tell that she felt sorry for me and that she disapproved of the circus people. But she scurried about, cutting the cake and pouring soda pop. My brother Elliot sat on the floor next to the humpbacked midget, trying to start a conversation. But Alexander turned his head the other way.

———

I liked this intern, Dr. Fishbain, better than the dignified specialists who examined Clarence in pieces from afar. I didn't even mind his green-haired wife. She wore thick glasses and was majoring in astronomy. Besides, she liked to visit Clarence. Dr. Fishbain was interested in Clarence's development and was writing a research paper about him. I did not object. Perhaps Rena came over to gather information or to experiment. That didn't matter. I could tell she liked Clarence. In fact, with her help and the assistance of Franz, Albert, and Ferdinand, we turned his bedroom into a playground. A big box of sand was installed. Then a shallow pool of water was added. It was all done to encourage motion. However, Clarence liked to lie motionless on the sand or in the water. He enjoyed it that way.

Dr. Fishbain and Rena tried to devise objects that Clarence would want to reach; "motivational elements," they called them. But Clarence's personality was such that only a few very specific things aroused his interest. He did not explore for the sake of exploration, like other babies.

I found out over a period of years which things he liked—feathers, mirrors, and tangerines. But I let them experiment. We hoped his leg muscles wouldn't atrophy from lack of use. And since he wouldn't crawl, we exercised them manually.

Sometimes, I became reluctant to leave my house. I do not know why. Clarence was no trouble to wheel around. It was fortunate that they visited during these periods. Rena said she would stay with Clarence if there was any place I wanted to go. But I couldn't think of any place I wanted to go.

—

Unfortunately the circus traveled, and the freaks reappeared only after long intervals of time. And some of them vanished, like the tall man or the humpbacked midget, Alexander. Ferdinand told me that Alexander used to cry a lot without any reason.

A POEM TO ALEXANDER,
THE HUMPBACKED MIDGET

———————

(*Written on the evening of Clarence's first party*)

You lie on the floor
Twisted like a gnarled root
Or something prehistoric
And ashamed.
(I recognize you.)
Dead leaves cover your tears
And the rocks you lean against
Glisten with salt.

How can I speak to you?

Can you climb where cold stars sing
Where the moon's metallic light is dancing?
(I think I would like to go too, sometimes.)

You lie on the floor
Twisted like a gnarled root
Or something prehistoric
And ashamed.

How can I speak to you?

With flowers falling on your back
And the sun wiping all your tears.
The rocks you lean against
Are fragrant with rain.

THE NEWSPAPER WOMAN

My hands used to freeze. But I'm a strong woman. My hands don't feel anything now. No cold is enough to freeze these fingers. But there is nothing to touch, just dry paper. He finally bought the newspaper stand. And a few years later he died. Here I sit touching the paper, part of it.

I see him in my mind, Carl, sitting here beside me. He knew things. His birth killed my husband. "What's the good of such a life. He can't be anything." So what. I tried to save money to move South. He would die early anyhow because of the rheumatic fever. But the warmth would have been better. That's what the doctor said. Lou didn't care. I wanted to go South.

It was a good spring, though, when they moved across the street. I wonder what happened to her. *Her* child lived. He might be dead now. She tried to be a good mother. But something was wrong. I don't know what, but watching from here with her door right across the street I saw when she didn't know it. At first I thought she was one of those unwed girls that you find in America. But when she came closer I saw that she wasn't a girl. Her eyes were old. She didn't look crazy—not exactly, though I heard from someone that she came out of an institution. You can't keep those things hidden. You could see it if you looked at her eyes sometimes. She was saying simple things, "How is Carl? Clarence got new shoes. The flowers are growing." But something else was going on all the time—something that set her apart and scared her. I didn't want to get too friendly with her. I have enough troubles. Maybe it was the son. How did it come? That was all I could think. And me with a Mongolian idiot for a son. How she even took him outside—I wouldn't if it was mine. God should forgive me, I suffered enough. Everything was all wrong. The shape of his head wasn't right, and it was bald except for a little piece of hair in the front. He would have been better all bald. And his feet were all twisted, turned facing each other. The crazy stare was the worst thing. I didn't want him near my Carl. But Carl liked him, and I saw it was good for him. Who else would play with Carl? It was an attachment; nothing to do with talking. Carl could talk. Clarence couldn't. Clarence made noises; terrible noises. My head used to ache. But I didn't mind him so much after a while. She kept him clean and dressed him up like he was a prince—suede jackets, tweed suits with red suspenders, felt hats of all colors and flowered ties. Well, I didn't have the money to dress Carl like that. He drooled over everything anyhow. I wasn't ashamed. I put a bib on him right in the street. I was saving the money to take him where it was warm. Maybe he would live longer.

She wore bright colors, mostly yellow and red. It didn't suit her. But she was a young woman. I think she hoped to find a husband. "Get rid of him," (God should forgive me) I wanted to say. It was the truth. She had a good figure. Not like the figure I had at her age, but graceful. The men came. I saw everything. But when they saw the child most of them did not come back. She had some peculiar ones; a tall thin man with glasses. He looked like a preacher. Carl said he had pictures of birds on his body. Carl didn't have sense enough to make anything up, bless his soul in heaven, so I knew it was true. She kept that one. She kept the queerest of the lot. And there were plenty of them. Not that I blame her. But I saw everything.

I miss them; or maybe I miss that spring and summer. It was like the last time I ever felt anything. Even then there wasn't much left in me to feel. You take a woman whose husband has hardly ever touched her, even when she was still young, and the warmth goes very fast.

We had struggled many years just for ourselves. No baby came. How could a baby come when he hardly ever put his seed in me, and a woman isn't fertile all the time. I wanted it. But I forgot it. I forgot love and a baby at last, thinking only of the day and the money. I liked to eat and put on a little weight.

Carl came when I was forty-seven. I guess peasant women keep their fertility longer than those born in the city. But what was the Lord God thinking of. Lou had a bad heart. When did he even come near me any more—those rare nights when we drank and laughed a little, pretending that the years had not gone. Lost in the past; king of his land, his manhood returned. It must have been one of those nights, when all of the seeds were pushed into me at once, that Carl was conceived. It was like a dance, a final dance before Lou settled into the earth. It must have been on one of those nights. In the morning he would wake up so weak but not wanting to show it. I saw it and tried not to look. I felt strong and young again. He would sleep most of the day, leaving me at the newspaper stand.

I should have had pity for her. But I don't have any for anyone. I used to pity myself when we first came from our village. Lou's spirit broke quickly. I had thought he was a strong man. But it wasn't so. He lost his manhood being treated without respect by so many employers who cared nothing for him. I lost my beauty very young. But now I don't change at all.

I think of her because she was young enough to have had another chance. (I don't know what went wrong the first time.) Yet she had none. And it was her own fault. God forgive me, I knew what I would have done if I had been as young as she was. But she didn't have the sense.

I don't think she saw how terrible he was with his sounds and his falling down, turning blue or jumping around laughing and then sitting with a crazy stare. Carl was the same all the time; sweet and quiet. It scared him when Clarence made loud sounds and danced around. And that there were never any words. Carl knew many words. But Clarence noticed when Carl was afraid and he quieted down. They sat here together, sometimes holding hands and kissing. It made me sick. I'm glad Lou didn't live to see it. It would have pained him more than his final stroke.

She should have put him away somewhere and never seen him again. Or even let him die accidently. (May God forgive the words of an evil woman who has suffered too much and too long not to see things as they are.)

When Carl died I wasn't surprised. I missed him. I still miss him. But mostly I think. I think of giving birth so late and of losing my husband soon after. And I think of the flowers that she had in the window. There was something terrible about the way they bloomed so fast, inside and outside the window. It seemed crazy. She never even watered them.

It makes me think how when God decides to make something grow in your womb, He does it even if it makes no sense or if the womb isn't so fertile. It doesn't matter if the thing He puts there is twisted, brainless, or barely human. It's just like that.

And there was a great wrath in the way those flowers grew.

THE SINGING WAITER (2)

Everything was different when Joe came. Other days were quiet. I wrote poems. It wasn't something that made me happy, but I had decided to become a poet long ago; when I was in college. Dead days, nothing happened to me there, and I didn't know what to do when I graduated. It was the same after that; living alone, writing poetry. (Some professor had said it was original and promising.) But I didn't plan anything. Maybe that was wrong. I took care of the necessities by doing proofreading. Sometimes I answered phones in offices or did clerical work. But I didn't really care about working. I wanted a husband and a baby. My sister-in-law said, "You go with the wrong type of men if that's what you want." She didn't understand that I didn't choose them. They appeared or they did not.

I wasn't unhappy. I was always writing poetry; it was about leaves and stones and stars. And I thought about having it published someday. I know I should have had more friends and gone out looking for things. But I didn't. In fact you could say that I was waiting right where I was for things to happen. And whenever they happened, I mean if a man found me somewhere, I didn't turn away. My brother's wife said I should be "discriminating." (I am, inside.) I have always had a lot of trouble with organization and with words. It even shows in my poetry. The words won't come out or I use the same words again and again. Many of my poems sound alike. The stones are small and metallic. And often they are frozen like stars. When these same images keep coming I sit and wring my hands or walk back and forth waiting for something new. This changed only when Joe came.

He came yesterday, his eyes lighting, invading the dead room. I catch things like that. He takes me out of this, my own silence. It is almost like magic.

Last night he let me read the part I love best; that of the mad Caligula. Usually Joe reads it and I play the woman, Caesonia, who loves him. But not last night. Oh, how I spoke; the words came out as my own:

"I live, I kill, I exercise the rapturous power of a destroyer, compared with which the power of a creator is merest child's play. And this is happiness; this and nothing else— this intolerable release, devastating scorn, blood, hatred all around me; the glorious isolation of a man who all his life long nurses and gloats over the ineffable joy of the unpunished murderer; the ruthless logic that crushes out human lives..."

Joe was astounded. "So you have rage and anger in you after all. Where do you hide it? Speak," he commanded, seeming to understand something within me that I did not know. I obeyed, trembling from the strain of all the words and feeling. "Be Nina in *The Sea Gull*," he ordered. I read:

"And there was the strain of love, jealousy, constant anxiety about my little baby. I got to be small and trashy, and played without thinking. I didn't know what to do with my hands, couldn't stand properly on the stage, couldn't control my voice. You can't imagine the feeling when you are acting and know it's dull. I'm a sea gull. No, that's not it. Do you remember, you shot a sea gull? A man comes by chance, sees it, and out of nothing else to do destroys it..."

I burst into tears, wanting to tell him. And Joe was kissing and holding me; the book of plays had fallen to the floor. "No more now, quiet," he said. I must tell you, I thought. "We will love and drink and dance," and in a crazy rapture we fell into the bed, my head spinning. I am pregnant. I am pregnant. But it was the wrong moment. And such a small reality was crushed by Joe's presence.

If only he could have stayed forever. But when I awoke, Joe was gone. But I had my voice, my tears, my anger. And I held them gratefully for a few days. I wrote well, I sang.

Then, as always, my life diminished and I became silent, accepting all; everything.

A POEM TO JOE

The mad silence of my innocence
Gripped to me, unconscious within
Not even a foot or hand is there
But growing, multiplying cells
Like ice-cold stars.
And what shall they feed upon
If you are gone and I am silent.
And what shall grow within me
But pebbles of disfigurement
If you are gone
And I am mute.

Raise the ax if that be necessary to awaken me.
I will submit.
But do not leave me now
When life like wildest leaves
Grows chaotically unwilled.

PLAYING

Other children fight, break pairs, and form new associations. It changes almost every day. Clarence and Carl are different. Their love arises every day more faithfully than the sun. And they are in each other's dreams at night. Although it lasts, this love is no more perfect than any other. There are the painful separations; days when Clarence cannot come outside, or Carl is running a mysterious fever. These days are dark. And Carl has learned the pain of loving two people who cannot love each other. When will his mother smile when she sees Clarence coming? Instead she shrugs her heavy shoulders and turns away, receding into her green stand. She is past fifty, but her hair is thick and black. It shines like a mirror in the sun. She braids it carefully, round and round her head; not a hair awry, not a speck of gray. Sometimes, for a moment, she looks like a girl.

When they want the same thing—a long stick, a piece of red cellophane to look through—they pull at it for a while. "Give me, give me," whines Carl. And Clarence makes a sound that pierces the air. I hear him from inside. Then one or the other lets go. It happens every day. No one has taught them. They discover every day that they can take turns looking through the pieces of cellophane they find on the street. Then they forget. But they do not forget for very long that being together is the important thing. Their tears and sounds stop quickly. Then they take hands and run somewhere.

When the bells of the ice cream truck ring out, they stand below my window. I give Clarence money. He understands. They stand aside until the other children have grabbed their pops and cups. Clarence holds out the money. "What do you want?" the man asks gruffly. Clarence looks at Carl. "Two," says Carl. "Two what?" They stare at him holding out the money. "Pops?" Carl smiles and reaches for them. Clarence gives the man the money. And they are delighted with themselves. Lost in pleasure, they forget, and the pops begin melting and dripping on to the hot pavement. They run to find a shady place to sit. Completely absorbed, they make a big mess.

Carl's mother appears with a towel and wipes his hands and face. She sees me at the window and quickly dabs Clarence's face too.

Now they stare into the air happily playing with the Popsicle sticks.

THE WORM

He had rolled down a small hill. I watched, smiling, holding someone's hand. Spring was here, and we could stay outside. Forsythias were appearing mysteriously, and the petals of the new magnolias were falling to the ground.

The man was reading a Sunday newspaper. Who? It could be any man sprawled out with the sun on his face. He was not unfriendly and asked if I wanted an orange drink. "Yes," I said, and he ran down the hill, not seeing Clarence, who was picking at the grass. I did not dream. I did not watch as he came smiling up the hill with two orange drinks. He breathed deeply and stretched before he sat down. "If this weather keeps up, we can go to the beach next Sunday," he said. I smiled and brushed an ant off his thick arm. What did I care about beaches, preparations, and next Sundays?

He patted my head and turned back to his newspaper. I remember the gesture. He hesitated as though he wanted something from me—a word, a kiss. I was looking at a tree. I remember thick arms with blond hairs, and tennis shoes. And that he wore glasses when he read. But I do not know who he was or his name. I would never be able to find him again.

Something happened that winter; something restless and unfocused was inside me. I couldn't write poems or read. I trembled once in a while for no reason. But the rest of the time I was serene.

The man had slept well, and I had made him breakfast; eggs flecked with parsley, and coffee. He looked healthy and studied every passing girl from beneath his paper. I didn't mind. I would prefer to have been one of them than myself, but the sky was pretty and the earth was warm. If he had left me and followed one, I wouldn't have moved. Nothing would have changed. I would have continued sipping my orange drink and watching Clarence at the bottom of the hill. He was pulling the grass out of the earth and making noises. The man looked up from his paper. "You'd better tell him to be quiet," he said, seeing people looking.

I went down the hill and sat next to Clarence. His hands were covered with earth. In the center of his palm crawled a small worm. His head was bent toward it but he couldn't find it because it was mixed with the earth. He made noises of surprise and pleasure, feeling it tickling him. I kissed him.

A small group of children who had gathered to observe Clarence had moved back when I came. It didn't matter. Clarence didn't know that they were watching him. They stared with big eyes and serious faces smeared with dirt. Some held sticks or toy guns.

One came closer. "Why is he all crooked?" he asked with some indignation. (The other children ran further away laughing.) I did not answer the question. "His name is Clarence, and he likes to dig and find things in the ground."

"Why is he ugly?" persisted the child. "He is not ugly, I said. "I think you are much uglier."

Then I went up the hill feeling the child's astonished eyes on my back. I lay down next to the man, knowing I had said something wrong. "Everything all right?" he asked, patting my hand.

"Fine. He's fine. He found a worm," I answered, closing my eyes to the sun.

ANY MAN

I feel rotten about the whole thing. If I had known, I wouldn't have gotten mixed up in it at all. Look, I have plenty of problems without *that*. There was no way I could have known. She was smiling, singing to herself. It was spring and she had on a yellow dress. It was the way you dream about it. She was walking along, smiling, carrying a bag of groceries. When I stopped her, she turned to me without any suspicion. It was as easy as that. Maybe it was too easy. That should have made me wonder. But it just wasn't something you think about. From the back you wouldn't think she was old enough to have a child.

Cheryl and I had just had a fight. This time I was getting fed up. I told her that I enjoy my freedom and that I'm not ready to settle down. Besides I was getting bored with her. But I was pretty depressed when she left. I didn't expect that. I was going to take a walk and think about the whole thing. Later I would call Cheryl and tell her that I missed her.

So I was walking when I saw her dancing along in that yellow dress. It made me feel good just to see her. I forgot Cheryl.

This is what I need, I thought, as we walked into her apartment; someone joyous and free who takes things as they come. "I didn't know there were girls like you," I told her. And I meant it. Then she told me she had a baby, but no husband. And she didn't seem bothered about that. I admired it. He was asleep, so I didn't see him until morning.

One night in bed with her, just like that, and I was ready to forget Cheryl. I didn't even care if she did it with everyone. Besides, she acted like she was crazy about me. She was a knockout in bed. But that wasn't the whole thing. Cheryl is good in bed too. It was that she didn't seem to want anything for it. She didn't ask if I had a girlfriend or a wife. She didn't even ask what I did for a living. The whole thing floored me. And I told her I'd never met anyone as wonderful. We didn't sleep much. I told her a lot of personal things; things I never even told Cheryl. Maybe I was afraid to. For example, I never tell anyone about my father who is in and out of alcoholics' hospitals all the time. I send money to him secretly, but I never see him. Cheryl thinks he is dead.

That night I confessed for the first time to anyone my fear of ending up like my father. I enjoy my liquor. But I'm already at the top of a big company. I pushed myself right up there, so I don't have to worry. And money means a lot to me.

She was very understanding. She told me that she writes poetry but it hasn't been published, and that she gets some money from a violinist who thinks he could be the child's father. Aside from that she works part time when her brother can take care of the child. I could see that she wasn't living so well, but it didn't seem to bother her. Nothing seemed to bother her at all. Yet she has a lot of depth. That's something I don't find in a girl very often.

I lay there wondering how it was that I never cared about things like that. I realized that I had missed something. How can I explain it—a kind of closeness with someone that makes you go deeper into the meaning of things. I hadn't had time for anything like that.

It was about the most beautiful night of my life. I felt so alive.

I asked her to spend the next day with me. We would go to the park with the child and then cook dinner together. She seemed very happy about it. I said too much. And I feel lousy about it now. I said, "You're one girl I'm not going to leave very quickly.

In fact, you'll have a hard time getting rid of me." I meant it. It was her fault too. She didn't tell me that she had a freak instead of a child. But to be perfectly honest, I think even that wouldn't have bothered me just then. Hearing about something and seeing it are two different things. I just wish I hadn't gotten into it.

I'm not the best guy in the world. But I don't particularly like to hurt women or take advantage of them. A lot of guys do. And they knock them all the time. I never talked against women. They have their faults, but basically I like them. I've never been out to give anyone a rough time. And I usually lay my cards on the table before someone gets too serious. Cheryl's a beautiful girl; passionate and not dumb. You can discuss things with her, and she knows how to be tactful with people. She isn't loud or lazy and can cook a decent meal. I didn't want more than that; not until that night. This girl was different. She seemed to understand the smallest things. And she wasn't spoiled. I thought with pleasure of the things that I could give her; things she never had. "I bet you've never been on a yacht, or taken a vacation on the Guadiana or the Gulf of Mexico."

In one night she meant so much to me that I tried to ignore the kid. Everything was wrong with him. He ate and walked—if you call that a walk—but he didn't know what was going on, and he made noises like an animal. She seemed calm about it all, so I was calm too, for a while. But he was deformed, and there was something about him that reminded me of a spider.

When we got outside I was ashamed. Everyone stares at him. She must know it, but she acts as though she doesn't see them. The children call him names and laugh. He cries but he doesn't know what they are saying.

Well, I began to fear that they thought I was his father. And that was too much for me. I walked with my head down in case I saw anyone I knew. But I put on an act for her. I still liked her, but it wasn't the same as at night. I didn't like her as much. If I was a real rat, I would have left then, but I had promised to spend the day. I usually keep promises. In fact, it's a principle with me. I did try. I patted his head and took his hand, but this made him shriek and act even crazier. The whole park was looking at us. Still, I thought I could stick it out. I tried to think of the night, but it got harder and harder. It disgusted me a little that she had given birth to something like that. I even felt annoyed that she paraded him around. But as I said, I put on an act. I held her hand, kissed her, and kept telling her how pretty she was. I began to wonder if she wasn't crazy, not putting him away somewhere. No one would have to know about it.

He went down to the bottom of the hill and started digging. I thought we would be left in peace, but he chewed the grass and ran in circles, falling and waving his hands. I was getting fed up. And she had to keep an eye on him every minute. I guess I have a cold heart. I began to hate her for getting me into it. The whole thing made no sense. I looked at her closely. She wasn't as pretty as Cheryl, and was older than I had thought. She sounded old when she talked to him. She also had a rash on her hands. I hadn't noticed it at night. But she was pretty. I had to admit it. Still, I began wanting to get away from the whole thing. I missed Cheryl.

If she had only said, "I know this is a mess," or, "It gets difficult at times," it might have eased things. Maybe I would have tried to help her. But she was always smiling and calm. I didn't understand her.

I could tell that the kid didn't want me around and didn't like me any more than I liked him. When I came near him, he put his head in the grass or flopped over in some crazy way. And when he thought I was going home with him, he ran away. I think he understands some things. I can't be sure about it because he does things for no reason most of the time.

Then he vomited. That was it. I didn't look her in the eye. Not after all those things I had said the night before. I made some excuse and got out of the dinner. I shouldn't have been there in the first place.

I don't know why it should bother me. It was just a one-night stand anyhow. Maybe that's all she wanted. I don't know. I guess I'll forget it. I'm going to marry Cheryl in a few months. Of course I never told her about this.

I just wish it never had happened. I try to pretend it didn't, but I can't.

THE DAY THE BIRDS FLEW

Birds were flying that day. They weren't big. There weren't very many, but I couldn't count them or tell their names. My eyes followed the circling, swooping movements they made. I tried to find the pattern. My head rotated rhythmically. I was enjoying myself. But Seymour looked disapproving. That spoiled it. He had good reason; he had come all the way from Pittsburgh to drive us to Jones Beach. "She needs to get out of the house more," Dr. Fishbain had told him.

Forsaking his daily practice, he came. He looked funny in his bathing trunks. They were delicately decorated with flowerlets and crescents. Uselessly he sat, his bulging stomach turning red. It was hot. The sand burned Clarence's feet. But he was afraid of the water. He held his ears against the sound of the waves like he did at home when the toilet flushed. And he wanted to sit where he couldn't hear them or see them rushing in, foaming with rage. Seymour was annoyed. We sat far back where there were no complete shells, only ground glass and small yellowish fragments. We touched them, Clarence and I. But Seymour kept his hands still. Without his violin, his hands were mute. We sat. Clarence ran back and forth, enjoying the pain the sand gave his soles.

I didn't see much—Clarence, the birds. I kept an eye on him. Seymour was afraid he would annoy people by his running, kicking up gusts of sand, sharp edges of shell.

I tried not to let on that I knew the others were watching me. You would never know it. Seymour had cautioned them. Yet it was obvious. All eyes were beneath sunglasses with exceptionally gaudy frames, or hidden under green umbrellas and large pink hats. No one looked at me directly. The men lay soaking up the sun with eyes closed and noses covered with white lotion. But they couldn't fool me for long despite Seymour's precautions. Occasionally I saw an eyelid slowly separate from the one below. The head did not turn, but the entire globe rotated in my direction. I trembled.

"Let's have a catch," said Seymour, holding our Clarence's yellow and red beach ball. Barely, barely, had I heard his plea.

"FUDGSICLES, FUDGSICLES," chanted a passing boy.

"Is he wearing the mask to protect himself from the sun?" I asked Seymour.

"Sh...sh...please...not here," he said noticing a head emerging quite boldly from beneath a green umbrella. Others were removing the disguises that had hidden their eyes; gaudy sunglasses were thrown aside in disgust. Pink hats were crushed with some violence. Seymour moved away from me and looked in another direction. He wanted to pretend he was not with me. I began to cry, not understanding why the Fudgsicle boy was masked, or why the others found me despicable. Even Seymour had turned away with shame.

But I held out my arms as Clarence came, kicking hot sand everywhere, sprawling over Seymour's red belly, punching it and laughing. Seymour got angry and pushed him away. Clarence had meant to play with the beach ball. I gave it to him, and he sat turning it around and touching the divisions of color.

"I am going to speak to him," I said with determination. "I'll get to the bottom of this once and for all," I said, rising, pulling down the edges of my bathing suit. Clarence was looking up at the strange birds. He looked afraid. I looked too, almost forgetting the "Fudgsicle boy." "Birds," I told him. He smiled, waving his arms and running to imitate their flight. He fell, closing his eyes and sinking forgetfully into the burning sand. I ran after the "Fudgsicle boy." Seymour went to get Clarence, whose nose was burrowing in the sand.

I pinched the flesh of his face, pulling at it.

"You nuts?" he said, backing away but too interested to leave. Others were staring with derision and mocking laughter beneath their disguises.

"Take off your mask," I said. A lifeguard held my arms as a circle began to form around us exactly as when a drowning person is finally pulled from the water. It increased. A swarm of unknown creatures awoke and came walking toward us as though hypnotized. I was afraid of them. Seymour arrived before I was completely encircled. "Come, we're going back to the car," he said, taking my arm forcefully.

"Clarence." Seymour explained that he was safe with some lifeguards who would escort him to the car. I submitted, walking automatically, following Seymour's steps. I followed Seymour over the burning sand, without thinking. Occasionally I glanced up at the birds who were still circling and swooping.

When his arm loosened I bolted away, falling in a deep cool shadow beneath the boardwalk. I do not know why. I did not plan to do it. The beach was crowded and Seymour's head turns so slowly. I hid behind a stone pillar that supported the boardwalk. There I dug a deep long hole and buried myself in it—all except my face. "No one can ever find me," I thought. "Not any of the masked people. I do not want to live among them any more."

It grew dark. Birds circled; fewer birds or else it was too dark to see them. Black came down all over, and wetness rose out of the sand. I shivered. And whispered, "Clarence." I whispered it only once. Then I forgot.

Patrol cars came flashing lights through the cold darkness.

They found me naked beneath the sand, squinting my eyes against the searchlights. They were silent, wrapping me in a blanket, carrying me on a stretcher into the back of the car.

"Home," I said. "Home." "Mother," I cried... but I spent that night and a few others in a general hospital.

———

A few days later, I signed myself into the institution. I did it surrounded by people who urged me. I did it myself, but I didn't know exactly what I was doing.

DR. HOVENCLOCK

I screamed when I saw my doctor. He wore a thick mask of synthesized flesh, a bad job with a fake moustache and holes to see through. "I hate you. Take that thing off." He'd heard about it and had thought up answers in advance. "I can't," he said with a studied earnest gaze designed to inspire trust.

"Stop playing with me. I see through it."

"Tell me about your childhood," he urged with a leer.

"Not until you remove it."

He sighed, dropping his cigarette lighter. He wished he was in bed with Lucille, the occupational therapist.

"Lucille, Lucille, Lucille, Lucille," I mocked. His eyes opened with amazement. "Who does Lucille represent to you?" he asked nervously.

"I don't believe in symbols," I said with spite. He lusted after more details but he was lost, impotent. I saw that at once.

"Look, you're only making things difficult for yourself," he said, trying to control his anger.

I laughed. I knew he wished our time was over. "Fifteen minutes and then you can get back to Lucille," I insisted.

Observing my mocking smile, he puffed his cigarette. He had decided to say nothing.

"That mask is putrid," I said.

"Time's up," he said, sighing with relief. An aide appeared at the exact second.

"Dinnertime," she sang. It was 4:30. "Isn't Dr. Hovenclock a darling?" She nearly swooned.

———

While we ate, we were watched by white-robed people who took notes from corners.

"The food is poisoned," said an old man gulping it down. "We all have to die anyhow."

I eyed the food suspiciously. There was a pleated cup of green mint jelly which scared me. "I hate green," I said softly. But the acoustics were good. A robed agent took it down.

"I HATE GREEN," I said louder, "G-R-E-E-N...GREEN UMBRELLAS, GREEN HATS, EYES, PARROTS, CUCUMBERS, GRASS."

She pretended not to hear but continued to write. I began to wonder whether or not she had a mask on. In order to find out, I threw the paper cup of mint jelly at her face. The other patients gasped. One or two walked slowly into their rooms. Someone laughed. The man opposite me continued eating the poisoned food.

I watched her wipe the mint jelly from her face. She wiped it too carefully, I observed. She is afraid her synthetic flesh might rub off with the mint jelly. She patted it dry, proving my point with her gentle dabs. She hid her anxiety expertly.

For throwing the jelly, I was judged a menace and put in a little room with a "special aide" watching me "around the clock."

"What clock?" I asked her.

"Oh, there are plenty of clocks around here," she said. "My name is Miss Pearl."

"Tell me," I urged, after we were on friendly terms, had played checkers and strip poker, "which ones are masked and which aren't?"

She thought for a while. "Truth to tell, they all look alike to me."

"Tell me," I commanded. Luckily for her, my doctor entered the room just then, smiling with his false face.

"Hello Dr. Hotcox," I said. (He frowned.)

"Why that's Dr. Hovenclock," began my special aide with indignation and sympathy for him. At a nod from him she left.

"Anything on your mind tonight?" he asked with studied offhandedness.

"Your ears," I said. "Where do you store them in the evening; in the ice box or in a glass of water?"

He laughed amicably. (I assumed that he and Lucille had just made love. No, not Dr. Hotcox...impossible.)

"I've always had these big ears. Unfortunately they don't come off." He pulled at them to convince me and to mock himself, hoping that that would make me like him. But I knew that they were fastened in a semisurgical way and would not come off without the precise formula. "They used to call me rabbit ears," he confessed, blushing.

"Too bad," I said. "The whole thing is disproportionate."

"Yes, what is?" he asked, thinking he was on to something.

"Your skull for example, your leg...and..." I laughed, looking at every inch of my Dr. Hotcox.

—

"I have a letter to you from Clarence," he said before he closed the door.

—

I opened it while Miss Peril sat knitting in a chair on my left. It was some circular scratches he'd made with white chalk on white paper. Punctuating these rhythms were random black dots.

"Birds," I whispered as I fell asleep.

LETTERS TO THE INSTITUTION

(From Ferdinand)

The circus just left New York. It was funny to be there without seeing you and Clarence. I thought of the first time we met. I thought of last year when Clarence met Josephine, the stunted elephant. Remember how he liked oiling her skin. I called Elliot to bring him down. He said that he didn't like crowds but that I could come over. I felt badly about Clarence not coming down to see the show. I couldn't get away. Some of our clowns quit and I had to double as a clown. I enjoyed it. I wish Clarence could have seen me.

When you get well I would like you to travel with the circus; you and Clarence. You both have a feel for circus life. It's different in the small towns but you'd get used to it.

I stayed at the Martinique Hotel. Most of the circus people stay at The Statler or The New Yorker because they're closer. I wanted to get away and do some thinking. The room was comfortable. I wrote a few poems late at night. They're not very good. Or else I did crossword puzzles. It's hard for me to fall asleep sometimes, and I had gas pains in my stomach.

I would have gone over late, after the show, but I know your sister-in-law goes to bed early, and I know she never cared for me even though she is polite. I figured that they have enough troubles without seeing me.

I sent you a silver elephant on a chain. I hope you like it. The doctor says he doesn't know when you can see anyone. I told him I was only in New York for a few weeks but he said you come first. I agreed with him.

By next spring I'm sure to see you and Clarence at the circus. But I will fly in and see you at the hospital before that if you want. Meanwhile I will be patient. Write me a letter if you have the time. Otherwise don't worry about doing it.

I send you all my love,
Ferdinand

(*From Seymour*)

I keep trying to see you or talk to you on the phone but the doctor says you are not ready. When will you be ready? I don't see that there is anything wrong with you. Anyone with a deformed child would have problems and hardships. Try to think of yourself while you are resting. You always dwell on Clarence. I think this separation will do you a lot of good.

I sent a check to your brother so he can put Clarence in a day nursery where there are other children like him. I know they don't have much money. I also sent a check to your doctor in case you want anything. I don't have many expenses here and I'm doing pretty well. I'm playing with the orchestra during the week and with the ballet on weekends. I don't like playing in the pit. And some of the musicians down there don't play very well.

I heard that there is an opening in the Cleveland Symphony Orchestra. I am going to try. Of course it means lots of practice. I wish I had more time for that.

I won't talk about the future now. I guess you're not ready to think about it. I think about it. Give it some thought when you have time. I want what's best for you. There is a rehearsal in a little while so I have to take a shower and get over there.

Try to cooperate with the doctors. I know they are trying to help. Let me know when I can visit you so I can arrange my schedule.

>Yours,

>>Seymour

P.S. Let me know if you need any money.

(From Elliot)

I spoke to the doctor over the phone. He says we can't visit you for a few more months. He said you are doing well. I know that you don't like him. I don't know anything about psychiatrists, but as long as you are there, try to talk to him. Sarah is doing a lot of reading about psychiatry so she knows more about it than I do. She read somewhere that you are not supposed to like him, and that it's a good sign that you don't. When I went to that psychiatrist years ago—I guess you remember—I didn't either like him or dislike him. Sarah says the name for that is ambivalence. She reads a lot. I wish it interested me more. Then I could understand what you are going through. I get annoyed when she keeps reading parts of the books to me.

I bought a goldfish and Clarence likes to sit right near the tank and watch it. Sarah bought a big magnifying glass in case he can't see it. He holds it and looks at the goldfish through it. Don't worry. He doesn't drop it. He also feeds the fish by shaking some fish food into the tank. Does he like cats? I don't but it wouldn't matter that much. Sometimes he has nothing to do.

We are trying to find a nursery school for him but so far we can't find one. When I bake cookies, he likes to play with the dough. I am not used to having anyone around during the day so I doubt that I'm good company for him. But he's no trouble. Sarah brings home little toys from the drugstore. She brought a little rubber ball but he chewed it and we were afraid he might swallow it or eat parts of the rubber. I told her to bring a larger one.

Seymour calls. We invited him for dinner but he said he is very busy with the violin. I think he wants to see you soon. That is up to you of course.

If there is anything you want we'll send it. We all miss you.

>Love,
>Elliot

P.S. Enclosed are some pencil markings from Clarence.

(*From Elliot's Wife*)

Everything is fine here. I guess we live a pretty dull life. Clarence adds a little excitement to our house. I think he is happy here. He eats well and enjoys playing with Elliot. Elliot's a child himself so they get along very well. I don't seem to have that easy way with children. Sometimes I think it's just as well that I'm not a mother. I just wish Elliot would get out of the house more. You know how he likes to lounge around. It really isn't good for the heart and the circulation. I know it's not good for Clarence, so we are arranging to have him go to a day nursery not far from the house. Elliot does take him to the park once in a while, but he needs more fresh air than that.

Ferdinand, that circus fellow, called. I tried to be pleasant but you know how I feel about that. What future is there in it for you? Despite Seymour's faults, he seems to be stable. And someone with an artistic temperament like you needs an ordered life. I hope you don't mind my saying these things. I feel I can be frank with you. Besides, Seymour is also a very fine violinist and yet he doesn't have the artistic temperament. He doesn't drink, chase women or squander his money, and he's loyal. You're past the age when you have to be madly in love to marry someone, and I think he has that on his mind. Don't reject him without thinking seriously about your future. You can't live the way you were living forever. You need someone to take care of you.

Tell your psychiatrist everything. That way you'll get better faster. I've been doing a lot of reading and I have great faith in psychiatry. I think the transference relationship is very beautiful.

We're getting Clarence a cat to play with. I'm not sure that he sees the fish. I think a cat is just the perfect thing.

Well, it's time for me to go to bed. Take care of yourself and don't worry about anything. This may be the best thing that could have happened to you even though it doesn't seem that way now. Oh yes, let me hear something of the therapeutic techniques they use there. Do you lie on a couch or sit in a chair facing him?

Love From All Of Us,
Sarah

CLARENCE'S VISIT

Because it was my birthday, they let Clarence visit me. Elliot brought him.

I waited for them in a huge wood-paneled foyer. Scattered about were patients trying to look normal; bathed, dressed, smiling wooden smiles. Visitors bent over them, whispering fake things; wanting to leave, forget, disappear.

They watched me openly now, without masks. Patients as well as doctors observed my actions continuously. Sooner or later they would discover what I had done. The fear of discovery kept me in a constant state of anxiety. But occasionally it diminished.

One patient in particular was discussing me in detail with a man who kept glancing at his watch. "I'm going to take you home very soon," he promised, as she wept against his chest. (I did not believe him.)

(What has your life to do with mine ...)

Reluctantly, he followed as she introduced me. We often walked together, gardened in a tiny plot beyond the porch and had long talks.

Her husband acknowledged the introduction with false warmth. He held out a manicured hand from beneath a folded blue serge coat and a felt hat. I said hello, smiling and looking as normal as I could. Visitors were always looking for hidden indications of aberration with glutinous curiosity. Besides, Dr. Hotcox was observing my social behavior from behind a paneled post as he pretended to converse with the father of one of his patients. I ignored him.

Miss Peril, my former "special aide," passed by, winking conspiratorily. At her side walked a girl who might have been me. It would have been better to have kept her hidden from these visitors; either bound against a bedpost or buried beneath piles of sand. She was unable to pretend. Emaciated, eyes terrified, she trembled as she passed.

The husband was saying how like a country club it was, and that he could use a little vacation himself. Laughing self-consciously, spying his watch, the foyer clock, the legs of a pretty visitor, he was a complete imposter.

But they pretended, kissing with a studied embrace. He feigned reluctance to leave, muttering how time flies, and that the briefs had to be prepared. (And the girl in his bed, I thought.)

—

"God have mercy on his soul," muttered an old visitor or patient, making the sign of the cross as Clarence ran bumping into everyone and falling into my lap. Elliot stood behind, holding a large white box.

I hugged him. It was as though we had never parted. And he went tumbling on the rug, shrieking and laughing. The old woman shook her head, muttering, as Clarence danced.

Elliot handed me the box and we sat talking quietly while white-robed aides looked on. "He's doing well at the nursery for the partially sighted. He plants radishes and does finger paintings. He hangs his own jacket on a hook. When he comes home he plays with the cat. Then we go to the park. He plays in the sandbox." I thanked Elliot for taking such good care of him.

Dr. Hotcox stepped from behind the post quite boldly, to meet Clarence. Clarence, my Clarence, tumbling on the flowered rug; braced, patched, dislocated, everything askew.

He began to tickle Clarence and to twirl him round and

round. It looked like a bizarre, ugly dance; a rape, a masquerade. I trembled with rage.

Clarence, deceived by Dr. Hotcox's charm, was captivated. "Feathers," he said as he was lifted high into the air. And he laughed.

I feared that he would take Clarence up the wooden staircase. Lucille would be waiting, and the three of them would disappear.

"Leave him alone," I shouted. I had forgotten the visitors who were chatting amicably while secretly delighting in my humiliation. Their sudden silence startled me. Could they know? I lowered my head and wept. Soon Clarence was beside me, playing with my shoes, and Elliot was holding my hand.

When I glanced up, I saw Dr. Hovenclock hiding behind a varnished balustrade. He looked hurt. Then he hid it, smiling with compassion. I hated his compassion. I hated him for hiding everything from me. "Who are you, Dr. Hovenclock?" I wondered. Then he disappeared.

Clarence, my Clarence, tumbled happily on the flowered rug.

"I do not like Dr. Hovenclock," I whispered to Elliot. Elliot looked puzzled, and said nothing. He gave me the white box which I had left on the floor. I took it indifferently.

"Thank you." I was very tired.

Miraculously Dr. Hovenclock reappeared. He said a few things to Elliot. Elliot put on his coat and then helped Clarence.

"Good-by," said Dr. Hovenclock, patting Clarence's bald head. I no longer minded.

From my window, upstairs, I watched Elliot and Clarence get into a taxi. I waved good-by, but they didn't know.

ZELDA

My roommate Zelda had had a lobotomy. But she remembered strange things with regret and realized that something had changed. "I used to play the harp so beautifully," she often said in a wistful tone, or no tone. She could not tell me any more about it.

Zelda was supposed to go to secretarial school every morning at eight, but she couldn't wake up. With what was left, the doctors (Dr. Hovenclock, in particular) were trying to assemble, to re-create a new Zelda. But shadows of the old Zelda could not be erased. She was melancholy sometimes, envying the complexities of thought about her, staring puzzled at the wall.

"Do you mind living with Zelda?" Dr. Hovenclock had asked. I had not minded.

"She's come a long way since the operation," Miss Pearl told me in confidence. "She had to be toilet-trained and everything, just like in the beginning."

But whatever they had stuck into her brain to erase Zelda hadn't succeeded. Something remained. Absently, she used to hum parts of symphonies, minor harmonies, and arias from obscure operas.

—

After Clarence and Elliot were ushered away, I came to my room to rest before dinner. Zelda was lying on her bed gazing at the ceiling. No one ever visited Zelda. Hearing me enter, she turned slowly in my direction. "What's that, a present?" she asked, looking fixedly at the white box. I shook my head. She sat up. I realized that she was waiting to see what was inside.

Without interest I broke the cord that was tied around it. One by one I held up each object for Zelda to see. There was a mirror from Ferdinand. When you looked into it your mouth became large, and your eyes small and elongated. (Clarence's room was lined with such mirrors from Ferdinand.) The mirror frightened me. I no longer looked into mirrors. But Zelda was intrigued. I gave it to her.

From Elliot there were some chocolate chip cookies that he had baked himself. Joe Paliacco, the singing waiter, sent a music box. It was a miniature stage. When the key at the back was turned, the curtains parted. A lady danced to the "Skater's Waltz," while an evil-looking magician grimaced behind her. "Joe wants to be a great actor," I explained to Zelda. But she was looking at her face in the mirror. Elliot's wife had enclosed some scented soaps that she sold in the drugstore. I gave one to Zelda, and she smelled it, smiling her vacant smile. "You have so many presents," she said. It was hard to believe that Zelda was thirty-eight years old. Often I wondered what she had been like before. "I used to be very sensitive." That was a sentence that she repeated at least once a day. I believed it.

At the bottom of the large white box was a small one. Inside was an expensive gold pin from Seymour, a violin. I never wear pins so I put it on my night table. "How cute," said Zelda, picking it up. "I once played in an orchestra." She said it as though someone had told her about it. I don't think she remembered. She put down the violin and the mirror. She lay back, staring at the ceiling as before. Each new thing or verbal effort made Zelda very tired.

She fell asleep before she saw what else was in the box. There was one radish in a paper cup. The name, CLARENCE, was printed on it in a style I didn't recognize. His teacher must have printed his name on it. That present made me happiest.

I put it on the dresser, in front of me, so I could see it from my bed.

LETTERS TO THE INSTITUTION (2)

(From Joe, the Singing Waiter)

Hello Sweetheart,

I miss you. Spring is bursting and blooming everywhere. I drove out to the country and picked dozens of wildflowers to remind me of you. I wish you had been with me. Sorry you didn't see much of me in the past six months. I had no idea anything was wrong. Sweetheart, come out soon and we'll go for a long walk all over the city and laugh and sing like we used to. You're the best lady to go walking with that I ever met.

Things are happening at last. Wish me luck. Some auditions are coming up for very important plays—on Broadway, but not commercial. I won't even breathe the names of the parts—things I've always wanted to do. Can it be happening at last? I have reason to think that I am practically in. But I mustn't be overoptimistic—not yet. I'll tell you the news as soon as it is definite. Meanwhile I'll be doing stock this summer just to keep in practice.

Come on honey, there's so much to live for, so much beauty everywhere, even when you least expect it. No more pain—a big smile for me.

> Yours Always,
> Joe

THE CIRCUS

The circus came every spring; before the institution, afterward, forever. It unified our lives. I cannot count the springs or separate the periods of our life. This interrupts the logical chronology of events. Not that they are of any importance. I prefer to destroy the natural sequences. I hate to count deaths or summers.

Even when I was in the institution, the elephants were dancing gracefully, standing obediently in a line with forelegs raised. I don't know why. Their bondage saddened me. Yet I liked their graceful movements and crumpled skin. In the end it was insufficient; that they wore pink garlands around their heads made no difference. Still they persist; the same elephants. If I went, I would recognize one from the other although they'd have grown. A paralyzed trunk, or one that whirled in the air for no reason, or a certain blemish on the foot pad. I know these elephants. They go on. That is the beauty of the circus.

There are changes, of course. They are like bruises. They never heal but a new layer of skin covers them, younger, shinier, but not the same; not having the resistance and elasticity of the old. It has happened to Clarence so I would know about it. He has lost many things. But he walks better, and his retina is no longer floating like gray film. With drugs his seizures are less frequent. But a flower does not make him laugh.

Circus changes amount to the same thing; the freak show was

discontinued. Perhaps the freaks were taught that it is degrading to be looked upon, particularly for money. They had enjoyed it before. Now they clown or ride the elephants. Alexander, the humpbacked midget, disappeared (Where is he?), Herman, the high flyer, broke his leg and became a clown, and Sylvia married an old shoemaker. Then she divorced him. She still jumps and dances; her small body covered with gay spangles. Honey is with her, but Ferdinand is gone. The changes are small. Sores heal. An elephant who dies can always be replaced. So can a midget. And Clarence still loves, though not as fervently, the sweet magnolia tree. He laughs less, examines things without absorption. These changes are not important.

The circus was always there. When we thought we had forgotten—let me think that my life never splintered. Let me pretend that Zelda, despite her lobotomy, is learning the harp. (Who is Zelda?) I want to believe, instead, in the jubilation we experienced the spring before I lost Clarence in the sand.

Everyone was worried; Elliot, Seymour, Elliot's wife, Dr. and Mrs. Fishbain. I heard their whispers. But they did not understand that before the extinguishing moment, or coexisting with it, are the heights of joy. If I said I was never as happy as I was that spring, they would remind me that I soon entered the institution. Perhaps it had something to do with my exposed nerves. I was susceptible—dying but mad with joy.

For three weeks we worked with the circus. I dressed magnificently and marched in the grand pageants with hooped skirt and shining wig. Lifting my leg in unison with fifty others, I pirouetted, waltzed, swung gently on ropes, and glided off the backs of bowing elephants. Ferdinand arranged it. And Clarence tended the lame elephant, Josephine. He oiled her body with salve and helped the circus veterinarian trim and polish her toenails. And in the final pageant, he rode on her back dressed as a clown. Josephine was covered with bells and wore a silver star on her head. Clarence wore a yellow suit with ruffles.

Seymour was furious, and Dr. Fishbain advised me to rest. It is true that I did not eat, and that I trembled. But never, never when I danced in the pageants. I needed no food or rest. In fact, I laughed and cheered the ailing clowns. Each clown, I discovered, had an impairment. A wooden leg was revealed, advanced sclerosis of the liver, heart murmurs. But they looked splendid marching and slapping their thighs with tambourines and cowbells; the children clapped and screamed for more.

Bells, stars, laughter. It was my youth, it was Clarence's zenith, that spring.

Elsewhere, in the supermarket, at Elliot's house, or in my own apartment the death of myself became manifest. I began to think that the women in the supermarket were wax figures. It amused me to think of them wheeling their carts with their children; blond wax dolls sitting among toilet paper and oranges. Clarence and I were real.

Occasionally it disturbed me, and I wanted to touch them to see whether or not they were alive. (The woman with the red bandana did not move when the bus stopped.) Sometimes, even when Ferdinand lay beside me, I imagined faces made of drapes, of shadows or of stains in the wall. They were laughing and staring at me. (What terrible thing had I done?)

To me that spring was the most fertile I can remember.

As soon as we arrived at Madison Square Garden, the mocking faces disappeared. I could touch the rough skin of the elephants, and wash Clarence's hands which smelled from the salves and ointments he used. Josephine loved him. She did not like anyone else's touch, and Clarence understood. He remembered everything he was supposed to do.

Nor did he shriek or vomit. And I have never been (before or since) more articulate. I flirted with the lion tamers and acrobats. My repartee was endless. It made Ferdinand happy. And I, amazed at the words flowing together without toil, let them spill, flutter out—well formed, uncensored, certain. Before and since

I have spoken haltingly, searching hopelessly for phrases with which to express my thoughts. It was a miracle, and it was contagious. Clarence spoke ceaselessly, chanting, "My elephant, my elephant," over and over like a prayer. I burst with happiness, hearing it. He had never connected two words before. He never did it again. It was something found and lost; a moment of promise—a blue daffodil that one thinks one has imagined seeing. It has to be accepted, because it can never, never be found again over the miles of earth, in all the clusters of bizarre and beautiful flowers in the world.

"You belong here," said Ferdinand, smiling. I nodded, believing it. And when he embraced me, Clarence passed by on his elephant with one withered leg in the air. Let me have that spring again. No. That would be asking too much. Besides, I could not afford it. It is enough that it flashes before me sometimes like colored lights and banners.

I didn't like it when Seymour waited for me at the end of a performance. My sequined gown, now hanging, glittered when I moved my head. I watched the spangles as I removed my golden wig and heavy eyelashes. "Look at yourself," he would say. And the gown disintegrated and lay silently on the floor. The mirror became the only reality. Vague, dilated eyes stared back, and a thin bloodless face pierced the fluorescent tubes. Behind this decaying face stood Seymour, his tie fluttering helplessly in the breeze made by a small fan.

Sometimes he took us home. I fell against his shoulder like an invalid. And in his presence I trembled, feeling all life and energy disappearing. Clarence fell asleep. The poisonous gases from the engine of Seymour's car choked us. (Where are the balloons that fly high, filled with helium and tiny pebbles? Have all the children broken them in unison, leaving fragments of colored rubber on the ground, crying, and then trampling them forgetfully?)

Ferdinand watched, still costumed, his tattoos glowing in the dark, and his face covered with luminous white paint. He waved as I drove away. "I will see you tomorrow," he was thinking.

In the apartment Seymour made tea and continued to chastise as I put Clarence's limp, sweating body into his bed. "I want you to be happy, and you act as though I am trying to hurt you," he said. His boxer shorts were creased and a dank smell came from his body. Even the cleaner could not remove the dry sweat that poured from his armpits when he played, and then became embedded in the threads of his jacket.

With an abrupt, heavy movement he jumped on top of me, panting, short of breath. It went on and on...unexpectedly and without desire, until with a muffled gasp he rolled off me and went to sleep. Glad to be rid of his weight, relieved that he slept soundly, I washed my face and body with icy water. Most of the night I wandered slowly from room to room, lost, my eyes adjusted to the darkness.

There was no one's name on my lips. And when I passed a mirror and pulled the small chain above it, my reflection frightened me. My heart jumped when I saw my face without wig or false eyelashes.

I sat on the couch. My fingertips ran over the rough material, feeling nothing. I touched one hand to the other for reassurance, but they were numb. (Who is this lady with the bandana?) Then I quickened my footsteps, not pausing, not thinking or trying to feel.

Let day come. So I can hide my face. I lit a cigarette but I could not feel the paper between my lips. I made sounds in my throat but they were also unfamiliar. For an hour, perhaps, and then it passed without reason. And I fell into the bed and slept for three or four hours.

He kissed my lips in the morning, and sat on the side of the bed lacing his shoes, breathing heavily, getting the laces twisted. "Well, I hope you're not going back there tonight," he said. "But you're old enough to know what you are doing." He watched as I faltered, unable to find things, confused because of his gaze.

"Play, Seymour," I said. It was the only way. And he did. The sounds filled the room, extinguishing everything; Seymour himself. They did not relate to his voice or thoughts, or to the clumsy body that had pounded upon me endlessly last night. His face changed a little; his features took form as he concentrated. His thick finger, hard at the tip, vibrated the string, and the bow jumped back and forth over the redwood. Clarence came running with delight. (His ears are perfect.) He listened intently while I made breakfast; eggs flecked with parsley, juice, and hot coffee.

I looked at him. Who was Seymour? Were those his fingers filling the room with beauty, and what had he to do with the man who deadened my body with his touch?

At last he shaved, patting sweet lotion on his cheeks. "Go away and do not come back," I thought as he promised to return a month later when his current series of concerts was over. "Remember, if there's anything you need, just call. Call me collect." "Thank you, Seymour," I said.

When he left, I wept with my face on the rough fabric of the couch. I muffled the sounds so Clarence wouldn't be frightened. He was playing in his room; in his sandbox, making mounds of sand like the homes of ants, and then breaking them.

I did not want to look at the green twenty-dollar bills that Seymour left lying on top of the refrigerator. I did not want to touch them.

SEYMOUR'S VISIT

Seymour visited me in the institution, bringing a bunch of wilted flowers. He was surprised to find me walking about. "You look fine," he said, as though someone had played a trick on him. He glanced around to see if anyone was watching before he kissed me. Then he glanced around again. He didn't know that behind the catcher's mask, on the baseball diamond, Dr. Hovenclock was spying.

We strolled together awkwardly until we reached a huge oak that defined the farthest limits of the hospital grounds.

Seated on the grass, he unlaced his black shoes with the concentration of a child. (The shoes were new and gleamed coldly in the sun, but the laces were frayed and knotted in several places.)

"I want to talk with you about something very important," he said without looking up.

"Strike one," called Dr. Hovenclock as one of the patients swung beneath the ball.

"I cannot remember things that happened recently," I told Seymour. "The shock treatments do that. But it will all come back eventually."

"Oh," he said with faked kindness and more annoyance. He did not believe me. "You look fine; the same as before," he said. Then he kissed me with deliberation.

He hesitated. "I want to marry you. We can all live in Pittsburgh, and Clarence can go to a private school. It no longer matters to me...I mean...the *others*. I've given the matter much thought. Whatever you did was not your fault. I don't care if Clarence isn't really my child."

My head hurt and I couldn't concentrate. I wanted to call Dr. Hovenclock. "Ball three," I heard him count.

Seymour looked nervous and uncomfortable on the grass. (I looked at his big belly and thought of it red and sunburned on the beach.) He had not succeeded in getting his left shoe untied. I tried to concentrate. "Others?" I tried and could only think of Clarence and Dr. Hovenclock. Finally I thought of Ferdinand. What did he mean?

"I will be here for quite some time..." Suddenly I forgot his name. Nor could I understand his intensity or what he wanted so badly.

I waved to Zelda, who was sitting on a chair sewing cross-stitches in a white towel clamped by a circular loop.

"Couldn't you give me some answer so I can get things settled?" he pleaded.

Answer? I didn't want to tell him that I had forgotten the question. I had had a shock treatment yesterday or maybe this morning. The lower part of my back ached vaguely. I couldn't think.

"Thank you for the flowers, Seymour," I said, glad to have remembered his name. He seemed distressed. Something was urgent. I did not like him very much. I don't think he liked me either, or believed that I didn't remember things.

———

The sun had gone down. Seymour had become silent. Then he put on his other shoe. An aide in white motioned for us to come toward the building. He stood up, breathing heavily, brushing the grass from the back of his wrinkled suit.

"I am not good at expressing my thoughts," he said. I tried to deny this. (He never had been.)

"You're a good violinist," I said, choking with invisible car fumes.

———

After he left, I requested that he shouldn't visit me for a long time. And when he called, they told him I could not see him; I don't know exactly what they said. He continued to send letters. I answered some of them. But I hardly ever thought of him.

———

The night he visited me I had screamed out terrible things against him in my sleep. Dr. Hovenclock told me. And I had awakened trembling.

ZELDA (2)

I had a lobotomy. I know that. They did something to me in a hospital. Dr. Hovenclock didn't do it. I asked him. He said it was done at another place. I don't remember it. I don't remember too much. He tells me things. He says, "Zelda, there are many things you can learn to do. It will take time." I hear sounds in my head and sometimes my fingers start to move a certain way. It is because I used to play the harp. "I want to see a harp," I said. He said that I would see one some day but that it isn't important. I hum things. I don't know where they are from. I was in an orchestra. An orchestra is where people play different instruments like the piano and the violin. I played the harp. But I don't know what a harp is. Someone told me it's pretty and has strings. They tell me things every day. I try to understand. I used to be very sensitive. That's what I heard my uncle saying to Dr. Graber. Dr. Graber is the director of this hospital. My uncle is busy. But he comes to speak to Dr. Graber sometimes. I didn't know what it meant, the word sensitive. I am starting to know what it means. I heard the aide, Miss Pearl, tell my roommate that she is too sensitive. She cries when people visit her. She cries because Clarence can't stay here. Maybe if she cries too much, they will give her a lobotomy. I don't cry. She knows a lot of words and writes them down. Dr. Hovenclock said she writes poetry. He told me about poetry and read some but I didn't know what it meant. I have a mark under my hair, but you can't see it. That's where my lobotomy is. I think Clarence has one because he has marks on his head. He is cute. He has no hair. I have hair. They are teaching me to set my hair. Everyone else knows how to set hair. They don't all do it. They know how because they don't have a lobotomy. I don't cry or laugh or yell like the other people.

I asked Dr. Hovenclock why my roommate punches her pillow and makes noises into it and twists her hands. He said she is upset and angry. I don't do things like that. I sleep a lot. I asked her if she wants a lobotomy so she can stop crying and being upset. She said that they give her shock treatments instead. Shock treatments are something else they do to your head. It makes you jump. They don't do it to me.

Dr. Hovenclock tries to find out who I like and who I don't like. But I don't know. I told him yesterday that I like Clarence and that I play with him when he comes. He asked me why I like Clarence, and I said because he is cute and maybe he had a lobotomy too. I don't think he knows anything either.

When you get a lobotomy it means you can't do anything. Then they teach you things. I wish it didn't happen because I am tired from learning so many things. And I wish someone else had one too. I would like my roommate to have a lobotomy.

I'm not sure if sensitive means crying and yelling or if it means writing things and playing in the orchestra. I know, because they all say it, that I used to be too sensitive.

A POEM TO FERDINAND

(*Written in the institution*)

To Ferdinand

The dream is dead
The elephant fell
(And the pageant's glitter fled)
Doors are closed to every bird
And purple leaves lie still.

How can I see, or guess
Which ropes to climb?
How can I know if far above
Among cold stars I'll twirl
Or fall back to the ground?

The ropes are far too high
The ground is pebbled snow
And if every elephant is lame or dead
Where are we to go?

Keep a star in your heart
No matter where I go
Go on and don't look back
Where lying on the ground
I see no rope, I sing no song
I say no prayer but wave good-by
To Ferdinand.

SEYMOUR SPEAKS TO FERDINAND

Ferdinand welcomed the bulky figure into his dressing room. Seymour sat with his large mouth open, panting and trying to catch his breath. Steps always left him breathless. His small strong hand took the hand extended to him and shook it. Ferdinand's long arm was decorated with canaries, snakes, and large veins.

"I'm glad to meet you, Seymour," said Ferdinand, smiling with long, stained teeth which tended to cross over each other, particularly in front. One side of his face was still painted with the luminous white paint he was using in his nightly performances. He continued removing the make-up slowly, hardly paying attention to Seymour, only listening to his heavy breathing.

"I don't know what to say," said Seymour from an old chair he had fallen into. He said it again. "I don't know what to say," staring at the crocodiles on Ferdinand's bony chest; fascinated and disgusted at once.

"I'm staying at the Martinique Hotel," said Ferdinand. "I don't sleep too well so I do crossword puzzles and write a little poetry. Maybe we could talk better there." His voice was even, slow and flat.

"No ... no ... this is fine ... I want to get things settled ..." He paused. "I'm a violinist." He felt silly for having said that.

Ferdinand continued removing the luminescent paint. "I've heard about it."

"I didn't mean to say that I'm a great violinist. I just play the violin." Seymour felt his cheeks burning and his thoughts becoming confused.

"We do the best we can," said Ferdinand. He hadn't yet made the transition from his performance. He was tired and wished to return to his hotel room.

It was silent and hot and no one spoke.

"I have so much to say," stammered Seymour. But he noticed that Ferdinand did not seem interested.

"Neither of us is good at talking," Ferdinand said slowly, smiling and turning toward Seymour. He put a tan shirt over his tattooed chest.

"But it has to be settled. I mean you know she's in the hospital. I went there, and she looked the same. But she doesn't know what's best for her. I've spoken to her brother. I mean, I'm worried and want to do the best thing. I didn't do it before."

(I really don't like doubling as a clown, thought Ferdinand, but they are short of clowns. I shouldn't feel humiliated about it.)

"And you know, Clarence is with her brother. And I don't really want to, but I'll take him too. I mean I want to marry her as soon as she gets out . . . they want me to also. I mean Elliot and his wife. I've been almost part of the family. I've seen everything happening." He looked at Ferdinand and waited.

"Everything takes time," said Ferdinand. His hands were trembling so he began tidying his dressing table; brushing off powder, putting the tops on the jars of cream.

"I have enough money to take care of her and the child," Seymour heard himself saying. "It isn't that I have anything against the circus." He looked down at his feet. Everything he said sounded wrong to him. It had always been so.

Ferdinand noticed that he wore a good suit, that his stomach bulged, that his face was smooth, round, and ashamed.

"You've taken good care of them, Seymour. I haven't been able to. You know we travel east, west, all over. It's my life. I can't give her the same things."

Seymour took out a handkerchief and wiped his brow. He didn't know how to go on. He felt sad that everything was so confused.

"I want to marry her," he said again, knowing it was the wrong thing to say.

Ferdinand felt very tired. "Yes, I understand."

"Then you have no intention of marrying her... that's what I want to get straight in my mind. I want to make plans. That's why I came to see you. I know you write to her. I didn't want her dancing in the pageants. It made her sick. She needs a home."

"You may be right. It all takes time. I have my dreams, but they may be all wrong. I've learned to wait."

Seymour did not understand. He wanted to say something and to get a definite answer. But he didn't feel he could.

He explained something about catching a train back to Pittsburgh and left.

"Clarence likes the elephants," Ferdinand said softly when Seymour was gone. Then he put his bony hands over his face for a few minutes.

If he cried, he didn't remember it the next day.

Seymour slept on the train with his chubby legs curled up under him.

Ferdinand spent the night doing crossword puzzles and thinking of nothing.

DR. HOVENCLOCK'S THERAPY

"On one hand," said Dr. Hovenclock, "you seem to be afraid that Clarence will be rejected. On the other hand, you have fantasies that he is being taken from you."

He was silent, wanting something. I watched the perspiration on his neck. His small office fan had broken.

"What are you thinking?" he asked gently.

"Of the dead bird," I said. (He waited, perspiring, saint-like.)

"He found a dead sparrow, bending over, stroking, feeling it, calling it 'feathers,' and he wouldn't go on."

"Then what happened?" Dr. Hovenclock had bags below his eyes. His facial pores were dilated from the heat.

"Nothing. That's all there is to it. You asked me what I was thinking and I told you, even though I don't think it makes any difference."

"Yes…" he said, thinking something I knew nothing about. "That seems to express your attitude about everything concerning yourself."

"What does?" I said angrily, sorry I had told him about the bird.

There was a long silence during which I felt like smashing his face, running out, crying, vanishing. But I had finally decided to cooperate so I might go home.

Softly, softly, as though he was whispering: "And you, how did you feel about the bird?"

"Me," I echoed. The word had taken my breath away. I trembled and stared beyond Dr. Hovenclock at the thirsty trees outside. I listened to the ping-pong ball going back and forth across the net and then rolling. Someone stepped on it by mistake. It cracked like an eggshell.

"You," he insisted, pushing the cracked shells into my flesh. "What did you feel about the dead bird?"

It was hard to focus on the bird. It hurt. "You look tired, Dr. Hovenclock," I said. There was only another silence. Dead bird. Me.

"I felt fear and disgust. I don't like dead things. I think I felt that. I didn't know I felt anything then. He wanted it. He cried and made terrible noises, so I put it in an old shoe box. There was one lying just off the curb. I put the bird into it and carried it around. Then we went shopping."

I stopped, waiting. Dr. Hovenclock was looking at the transparent paperweight on his desk. He fingered it. There was a dark look on his face.

"Who are you judging," I yelled. "What is so terrible about taking home a dead bird. What right do you have to condemn me, you false psychiatrist."

The clock ticked in the hot room. The ping-pong ball had acquired a form and was popping over the net, very much in danger. Dr. Hovenclock's eyes were closed. His face had no expression. He might have been dead, or a wax replica of Dr. Hovenclock . . . I stopped this thought abruptly. Months and months and still it would suddenly arise.

"He liked to touch it, to put it against his cheek, and carry it from room to room. I saw that bugs were eating its eyes. It was putrifying. But he had grown attached to it. Finally, it smelled and parts of it were greenish. I had to throw it away. (I started to cry unexpectedly.) He wanted it, and didn't understand. If I could have kept it, I would have."

"Wouldn't it have been better if you had never picked it up in the first place? You could have thought of what would eventually happen." He said this quietly. Yet he awaited my answer.

"No," I said. Perhaps he was correct logically, but he didn't know how little there was. How could he ever know about a dry universe of empty pebbled streets.

"There are so few opportunities for his happiness. I know you don't understand, but..."

"And yours?" He interrupted, blurting it out, sending the fragments flying through the air again. The even rhythm of the ping-pong game had stopped. It was airless outside; thick, heavy, threatened by a storm. Black outside his office window. No trees. The dead fan looked menacing instead of useless.

The fool, I thought, looking at his averted face. He couldn't know that each day began and died, that tomorrows were just illusions for Clarence and me. Could one afford to refuse a dead bird?

I became silent, recognizing the vast space separating Dr. Hovenclock from myself.

The rain began with sudden flashes of light. For a second I saw the hidden world betrayed by his lined forehead and the hollows of his cheeks. Someone of flesh and bone appeared in his chair.

—

Once a month, the head of the institution, Dr. Graber, called me into his wood-paneled office. Peering down at me from an enormous velvet armchair, his lower parts hidden by an impressive desk, he would ask, "And how are the masks?"

"Gone," I answered. I did not mention my passing thought that he himself was motorized with a tape recorder embedded in his abdomen. Nor did I reveal a sudden obsession about the constituent elements creating the agonized grimace of a new patient. These preoccupations did not last long. Besides I wanted to return to Clarence.

"Remember," counseled Dr. Graber, "we can only help you if

you are truthful with us. An occasional relapse is to be expected."
He stared at me waiting for a confession.

"So far, I have had no relapse," I smiled.

"Good," he said with enthusiasm. I don't know if he believed me.

—

Here even more than outside, I learned the value of pretense.
That was the only way back to the world. In the beginning I confided my fear that an individual wore a false nose or eye to a friendly aide or to a fellow patient. Somehow the information traveled to Dr. Hovenclock. Quickly I became like the others. I confided nothing that seemed bizarre. Instead I socialized, laced wallets, and tooled change purses in Occupational Therapy. I made four bookmarks, three enamel ashtrays, a mosaic coffee table with a black flower in the center, and wove a complex pattern of rope around the frame of a stool for Clarence. I looked at everyone pleasantly and openly while fearing yet—fearing forever the appearance of a synthetic face.

And I am sorry now for what I did not say. It was my chance to tell them about my hands. But how could I? Besides we were sidetracked by the masks. I never even whispered quietly about the welts. It would have been the end, I thought. It might have been. But it wasn't my fault.

Dr. Hovenclock watched my activities and admired the things I laced and wove. But he was clever enough to persist. Why was he not clever enough.

"Let's get back to the masks," he would begin.

"I don't see them any more," I protested uselessly.

But he liked their symbolism.

"What are you afraid of finding out about yourself?" he asked many times. (I thought he was on to it.)

"Nothing. And the entire subject bores me to death. There's nothing I can find out that I don't know already."

"That's true in a way…" he agreed, taking me by surprise.

"You seem to know all about the deceptions of others; their frailties, lies, and hypocrisies. You also know about your son; his every gesture has meaning to you. You know what he needs and what he wants...but what do you know about yourself?"

That's what it had come to. Each time I saw him, he hammered away at that question while I wrung my hands together.

"With a knife," I once thought, "you could remove them," but I said nothing.

"What do you know about yourself?" His office was whirling. His new fan lifted papers off the desk, turned them upside down, creating a chaos I could not stand.

"You're a pawn," he shouted above the whirling and buzzing of his fan. "There is no you," he accused again. I swallowed my rage as the fan lifted me into the air and sent me spinning to the ground.

"Fine technique today," I said, as I was whisked out.

———

But I thought about it secretly, lying awake while Zelda snored heavily and forgetfully. According to Dr. Hovenclock, health meant wanting things. What would I have to pretend to want before he would let me leave? I longed to return to Clarence. It was too late. I could not begin to create real desires. I desired only to be with Clarence. But that was the wrong answer. He wanted me to desire as if Clarence did not exist.

A husband? I wanted a father for Clarence. But for me? "You." That's what Dr. Hovenclock kept saying. He was right. I did not know myself. He wanted me to extract Clarence; to become I instead of we. Never.

Show me, Dr. Hovenclock, in this world where snows melt, rain stops, people love and hate in the same day, meet and part forever in a month, what there is to want. Show me a different world, if there is one. Show me your world or else leave me with mine. For who am I without Clarence?

And if the masks return I will know it is because I would not find out why. Only I know certain things. I made my choice not to know. And this choice created who I wanted to be. It was hard. It was wrong. I could do no better.

But in the mornings I lied. I told Dr. Hovenclock that I was thinking of what I wanted for myself; as though Clarence did not exist. He showed great pleasure.

Night was my time of rehearsal. "I never hear you say, I want this or that," he had said almost from the beginning. Now he heard it. "I want to publish my poetry. I want a man who cares for me. I want friends I can talk to. I want to learn languages— Italian, Russian, Greek. I want to dance. I want to live."

I wanted nothing but to sit in a restaurant with Clarence; to hear his voice, to know that we existed together.

Occasionally I looked at him while I was reciting the things that I wanted. He was smiling. Did he understand that these were only false desires?

But I repeated my desires so often that I no longer was sure whether or not they were false.

"Zelda," I asked one evening before dinner, "what do you want most of all when you leave?" She laughed her hollow laugh. "I want to be the way I was before I went to the hospital. The doctor says I can't." Then she rested on her bed, soundless, staring at the ceiling.

THE DAY I CAME OUT OF
THE MENTAL INSTITUTION

———————

The day I came out of the mental institution, Ferdinand called. I had been pacing about the apartment, not even opening the windows. (They had been shut tight for two years.) But I preferred the musty smell to a spring breeze which might startle me. The kitchen sink was overflowing with fantastic moldy growths from pieces of lemon and tea leaves that had changed. Now and then I studied the molds which were blue and green. It did not occur to me to remove them, or to dispose of my geranium plant, which had become a dry black stalk.

I stared at things, not connecting them; an old blond wig covered with soot, a red and yellow beach ball, a pair of men's socks, three bells, a broken hat with polka dots, and a box of feathers overturned.

I should have cleaned up and opened the windows because Clarence would be coming home at three.

"Ferdinand, I don't know where to begin, or what to do," I said right after he said hello.

"I am at the Martinique Hotel if you need me," he said. But he did not insist.

I thought of his body covered with gorgeous dinosaurs, lizards, and dragons with flaming nostrils. The hair on his chest is a forest for camouflaging salamanders, insects, and dangerous snakes.

I described the fantastic budding mold and told him about the way I could not even sit down. And that there were false eyelashes stuck to the mirrors.

"The circus is in Florida, but I am here on the fifth floor of the Martinique Hotel," he said. "I am writing poems and doing crossword puzzles."

It helped me to know that Ferdinand was near. I was surprised too, because he was supposed to be traveling through the southern states with the circus.

—

The door was not locked. Clarence came in without a sound. Then he laughed. When I turned around, he was laughing and kicking up his skinny legs. In his hand was the bottom half of a milk container with three small radishes growing inside. Delicate roots came from a hole punched in the bottom with closed scissors.

He held it up to my face, and I smelled the black, over-fertile soil that he had patted so carefully with a spoon. (I had kept the container that had held a single radish long after the radish turned to dust. I had packed it in my valise when I left the institution.)

I smiled and touched his hair—a mound of fuzz that came up to a rounded point in front, just above his forehead. The back of his head did not grow much hair. Once in a while a small tuft appeared and I was hopeful. But in a week or two it came out. I used to find these tufts in Clarence's bed or near some toy he had been playing with.

Clarence had visited me at the institution almost every Sunday during the past year and a half. Before that I wasn't permitted to have guests. Besides, it was hard for me to remember things then, because of the shock treatments. This year the doctors had a conference and decided not to give them any more. Instead, I swallowed a multitude of small pink pills called Tofranil. I took them every day, together with a brown iron capsule and a flat green pellet.

My brother Elliot brought Clarence every Sunday. Elliot is not sick, but he never found out what he wanted to do for a living. He stays home reading or watching television while his wife works at the cash register in a drugstore. She doesn't mind, because Elliot is good to her. Besides she can't have any babies.

For two years Clarence lived up in the Bronx with Elliot and his wife. He attended a day nursery for partially sighted, retarded children. (This was the only nursery that would take him.) Elliot didn't know what to do with Clarence all day. In school he planted radishes and played with water in a big plastic tub. He also made finger paintings.

Although Clarence can see color, he had done all his paintings with black paint. His teacher had printed his name at the bottom of each, rolled them up, and tied them with a string.

We broke the string and sat on the floor looking at his paintings. Each had the imprint of his palm or fingertips. He was delighted with what he had done and made a lot of noise. When I taped them to the wall for Ferdinand to see, Clarence danced in little circles.

Then I took my Tofranil and lay down to rest. Clarence touched my face with his thin fingers and sat down near the bed.

———

I awoke and looked at the ceiling. I struggled, but the room was blank. (The names of things would slip away sometimes, Dr. Hovenclock had said. But in time it would happen less.)

I trembled, waiting. My eyes rested on his open palm. The fingers pointed toward the sky. The other hand covered his face.

He awoke and rubbed his eyes. "Mommy," he said before turning to me. I began to cry because I could not remember his name.

———

Ferdinand wore a scarf with yellow flowers. I think I once gave it to him, but I am not sure. After supper, which he brought in a paper bag, Clarence rode on his back giggling and waving. Obligingly, Ferdinand crawled around the apartment.

Then he put on his rimless glasses and read from the writings of Mary Baker Eddy. He was a devout Christian Scientist. And he still hoped that the psalms would heal Clarence and me. I listened politely without concentrating. Clarence, wearing his own thick glasses, sat on Ferdinand's knee. He liked Ferdinand's voice. Once in a while he bent his head so that his glasses touched the book. But there were no pictures there. He went into his room and brought out a book of elephants that Ferdinand had given him many years ago. Holding it close to his eyes, he made sounds.

Ferdinand sat alone in the center of the old sofa. He looked very big and lonely. But what could I tell him? If I told him about the year when I hardly existed, lying there or walking up and down seeing masks, he looked puzzled. He didn't want to know too much about it. He just continued traveling with the circus; east, west, or wherever they went. Although he was solitary, and sat sometimes, remote, with his hands folded looking at the carpet, he was content to go on. Not like Joe, the singing waiter, who jumped out of a window after failing an important audition. (I heard about it because there was an article in the *Times*. Otherwise no one would have told me.)

———

I was still confused, so Ferdinand gave Clarence his bath and put him to bed. Then he cleaned the sink and opened the windows a little. The spring night came in.

"I'm afraid," I said. He patted my hand. We drank coffee and ate the almond chocolate bars he had brought for me.

"I have a nice room at the Martinique Hotel. It's quiet so I write poems and do crossword puzzles. But I'll stay here tonight."

He meant he would sleep in the big bed with me like he used to and make Clarence's breakfast in the morning. I didn't want him there, but he had left the circus to come East and wait for me. (Even when I was in the institution he wrote me letters asking me to marry him and travel with the circus.)

He held my hand underneath the cover and did nothing else. I slept all right. When I awoke he was still sleeping so I studied my favorite tattoo; the blue dragon.

Clarence came into the room with a lemon cut in half. (He thought it was an orange.) When he saw Ferdinand in the bed, he laughed and danced.

—

The morning after my first day home it was sunny. When the bus took Clarence to school and Ferdinand went back to the Martinique Hotel, I dusted. Then I washed the windows.

DR. HOVENCLOCK

I was forty-five when I came to this psychiatric hospital. My wife had left me; not that I blame her. I'd been a successful internist for many years. We lived well, and our nine-year-old daughter was learning French at a private school in a Connecticut suburb. Everything was established and impeccable when I suddenly made the decision to become a psychiatrist. I had thought of it while I was in medical school, but I met Audrey in my third year, and we made plans. Audrey knew what she wanted, and I wanted what Audrey wanted. I was young and very much in love. Nothing really changed as the years passed. But I felt that something within me was incomplete. I laugh now, or at least smile, remembering how hard I tried to convince my wife that I had something important to "contribute."

There's no point going through the details of that struggle. I've always had difficulty making decisions. But this time I made up my mind and went through with it.

My first patients at the hospital were easy ones; what they call short-term patients. Something quite definite had occurred in their lives, and they were temporarily dysfunctional. The death of a husband, or mother, an unwanted child, the loss of a job caused many of these upsets. I think these patients would have gotten better without my help.

I was quite excited when I heard that Dr. Graber, the head of the institution, was giving me a severely psychotic patient who suspected people of wearing masks.

I disliked her immediately, even though I told myself that her behavior resulted from her illness. Perhaps it was because she called me Dr. Hotcox. I hated that name, and the other doctors teased me about it. For two months I made no progress with her. She would tell me nothing. And I felt that the other residents could have gotten much farther by then.

Without telling Dr. Graber, I decided to visit my psychoanalyst, Dr. Weilbach. "So you're having a bit of trouble," he said when I told him I was going to give up this patient.

"Look, Dr. Hovenclock," he said, "I'm going to be very direct with you. I thought you would get by without going too deeply into personal philosophy, but I see I made a mistake."

Then he told me to get off the couch and to sit facing him. This surprised me because Dr. Weilbach was, I had been led to believe, a devout Freudian.

"I know some of my hostile feelings toward my patient have to do with my marriage, rather ex-marriage," I said.

"Yes, yes. She is manipulating you just as Audrey did." I protested in vain that Audrey had not manipulated me.

"Dr. Hovenclock, I will be very honest with you. You are forty-five years old and still you don't know who you are. You are a puppet."

"You must be senile," I said, surprised at my own anger. But he just smiled.

"The decision to become a psychiatrist was the only free decision you made. But it is not really free. It is your way of trying to find out who you are. This patient calls you Dr. Hotcox and you cannot deal with it. Why? You tell me why."

"Well, Audrey didn't leave me just because of my decision to become a psychiatrist. Sex never worked out with us. I never could satisfy her. And there was a period of two years at the end when I became impotent. I should have told you that before."

"Yes, yes. A puppet cannot satisfy anyone; wife or patient. All puppets are impotent in some if not all ways. Think. Who is Dr. Hovenclock? He is someone being born or trying to be born at the age of forty-five. No shame in that. But face it. See it through. Don't abort."

"I don't know if I understand you," I said.

"Oh, I'm sure you do. And you will understand your patient; all your patients are people who have aborted at some time. You must help them give birth to themselves. You are the instrument of that creation."

"I don't know if I can do it."

"Not if you are not born yourself."

"And how do I suddenly emerge?" I asked with sarcasm.

"You can begin by wanting, being, doing, committing yourself totally. Begin with this patient. She senses your psychic impotence and calls you Dr. Hotcox. Take a firm grasp on her."

"I'll give it some thought, Dr. Weilbach ..."

"Give up this patient and you give up Dr. Hovenclock and become ex-husband of ex-wife, Dr. Hotcox, or whatever any puppeteer wants to make you."

It took me a while to calm down. But I decided to help the woman give birth to herself while I was emerging very late, from the passive foetal position myself.

"Dr. Graber," I said, "I want to work with that patient. I am not as fast as the others, but I think I can help her." He was delighted.

—

The situation improved after that. I no longer resented her, and she soon began calling me Dr. Hovenclock, and when she reverted to calling me Dr. Hotcox, I was able to accept it.

—

I began to notice that she never said, I want, I think, etc. It was always "we," or "Clarence and I." So we had the same problem. I struggled to create a structure within her that was independent of Clarence. At the same time I didn't want to threaten her too much by making the psychic separation too abrupt.

When I called her a pawn and told her she didn't exist, she reacted much the way I had reacted when Dr. Weilbach called me a puppet.

"And the masks?" asked Dr. Graber.

"She has so withdrawn into this world of Clarence, her son, that she has no reality to herself, hence others are flat and unreal to her."

"I think there's more to it than that; definitely a paranoiac aspect," he answered.

"I'm trying to get at it. She is obviously afraid that something about her will be discovered. It could be guilt about having a defective child, guilt about almost having an abortion, or ambivalent feelings about Clarence."

"You just keep on with it," said Dr. Graber. "I leave her in your hands."

———

"Dr. Weilbach," I said, "I do not understand why she is always accusing me of sleeping with Lucille, the occupational therapist. I hardly speak to Lucille."

"And your patient's insinuations make you angry, Dr. Hovenclock, or should I say Dr. Hotcox?" he answered.

"I see that name doesn't bother you any more. You know you can learn much about yourself from psychotic patients. She is trying to tell you something. Maybe she senses that you cannot relate to women in a masculine, aggressive manner. That threatens her transference with you. And perhaps she senses that you are attracted to Lucille, and even fantasizes that she is Lucille. There are many possibilities if you continue to examine yourself."

———

Dr. Graber thought it was too soon to let Clarence visit, but I insisted strongly since it was her birthday and I had been hammering pretty hard at her creating an independent self.

During the visit she had a fantasy that I was taking Clarence away with Lucille. Once again I was puzzled and lost confidence in my judgment. It had been too soon for such a visit.

I could understand her fantasy that I was taking him away, since I was in some sense trying to separate her ego from his. But where did Lucille fit into it?

"Dr. Hovenclock, it was a perfectly predictable reaction," said Dr. Weilbach in the semi-harsh direct tone I'd become accustomed to. "I told you that your patients will sense your inner changes, even though they cannot relate in a realistic manner. She senses a growth in you, and that now there is a real possibility that you will be able to form a relationship with Lucille. She is acting normally jealous and threatened; on a paranoiac level, but not far from reality."

"As a matter of fact, I have been planning to ask Lucille out for dinner on my night off."

When I think back to that first important patient, I wonder if I went far enough. I realized that it was too late for her to create an entirely independent self, just as it was too late for me to go back to my very beginning. We must accept some things as they are. She hadn't seen the masks for three months. I think she was telling the truth, and I couldn't get at whatever guilt had caused such withdrawal from other people.

"Dr. Graber, I see no point in keeping her any longer. The anxiety that caused the masks has apparently diminished. She has chosen to take care of her son, even though there is some question in my mind about her capacity to do this. Yet I feel that a patient should be autonomous about basic decisions."

"It is a cliché, of course," said Dr. Graber, "but true all the same. We know very little. I don't think she is ready to leave. However, I have been wrong before, and I have been guilty of keeping patients too long. What bothers me is the time she caught her hand in your office fan."

"That was a long time ago. And it was just an accident."

"That may be so, Dr. Hovenclock, but are you sure there was not something she was trying to tell you by that so-called accident?"

"Look, anyone can get their hand caught in a fan. I don't believe that every little movement and slip of the tongue has significance."

"I respect you, Dr. Hovenclock, but I disagree with you there. I am an old conservative. I believe that everything is a revelation."

I wanted to consult Dr. Weilbach about that conversation with Dr. Graber. I hadn't seen him for months. When I called his office, I was shocked to hear that he had died a few weeks ago.

Dr. Graber left the decision to me. And I made it as best I could. I made it knowing there were some things I did not completely understand. But I felt I could do no more.

———

I think about it often, although I have had about one hundred patients since then. I think of the birth I went through by the brusque but knowing hands of Dr. Weilbach, and I can only hope that the delivery I tried to accomplish was reasonably successful.

MONOLOGUE TO ANY MAN

You are asleep beside me. My eyes are open. I stare at the ceiling—its familiar stains and cracks do not comfort me. There is a loneliness in me beyond thought or words. It is like being very hungry in the morning, or like falling through endless space. Nothing surrounds me. When I glance at you I feel tenderness. My fingers touch your cheek lightly; I kiss you. But the ravaging within me continues.

I did not feel that way when we fell asleep. I felt secure in your arms, relaxed with your love-making. You whispered loving words that I knew were not lies. I fell asleep peacefully a few seconds after you did.

But it is different now. None of that is left. I tiptoe out of this room and glance at the clock which ticks softly in the kitchen. It is 4:45. I lift the kitchen window briefly to taste the mist outside, then I glance about in the gray darkness from object to object. They are strangely tense and illumined by threatening light.

Clarence is breathing heavily from his mouth, his legs crumpled and his head bent against his chest. I watch his sleeping. "Clarence," I whisper. (I do not know why.) Then after glancing in a few mirrors, I come back into bed. Your sleep continues indifferently, undisturbed.

(What has your life to do with mine...)

I turn on my side to watch. I have felt alone, I have been alone. The thought of morning increases it; relentless, icy cold, without mercy—a new day. When things are clear and stated, they do not bow to a tear. Why cry?

It is funny how I know when someone is leaving. This knowledge exists now. Despite the love-making, the arms holding me like steel bands that say forever, I know. Maybe that is part of the reason I know.

It was a lovely evening. Clarence sat on your lap, and you read him a story, holding him close. And he fell asleep there. Kissing my neck, you put him to bed, closing his door lightly and returning. There was a new tenderness in you tonight. And Clarence slept well.

Then I read you some of my poetry. It is not very good, I know. But you listened, looking at me with fondness, love, and a tiny element of something you did not know. I did not know.

Diluted, hidden, I sensed its lethal quality without awareness. With the tenderness, a distraction, like someone watching a loved one from afar.

And that is how you loved me tonight. With the old motions, an added passion, a painful tenderness.

I know it now, with dawn in my eyes—that your love with all its strength and passion was dead. What seemed overalive was the final symptom of love's death. I wish I did not know.

I will not ask why.

———

The secrets of your heart are yours. And the loneliness beyond the reality, beyond the nearness of your body and the love in your eyes, is mine.

THE MAGNOLIA TREE

I don't know where Ferdinand is buried. Clarence and I planted a small magnolia tree in his honor.

Sundays, elegantly hatted, we walked through the stone tunnel, around the duck pond to our secluded plot. We carried bent watering cans from our circus days when Ferdinand taught Clarence how to bathe the elephant. If it had been a dry week, we sprinkled water beneath the tree. We watched the roots suck it inside. Then we wet the blossoms which were always about to fall apart.

The eagerness of the magnolia to bloom and die made us respond to its slightest need.

Clarence was fascinated by the petals which lay at the base of the tree. No matter how brown the edges had become or how dry, he pushed them back into the earth. He thought each one would produce a tree. I am sure of it. (When a dead petal crumbled in his palm, he blew the parts away.)

Although he had planted seeds many times, he did not conclude that flowers did not grow from petals. Rarely was Clarence able to make generalizations, or come to conclusions. This caused his happiness. But at other times it made him seriously vulnerable.

—

It was particularly windy one Sunday, and petal after petal dropped from our tree. He did not want to leave. He would have pushed the dying flecks beneath the soil all day if I hadn't been there.

Reluctantly he agreed to run after the pigeons on the terrace of the Zoo Cafeteria.

Sedate in his olive green jacket and crimson tie, he waited for me to return with rolls and plates of bouncing Jell-O. He liked to put his cheek against the Jell-O or stick his finger into it. This made him laugh.

Returning to our table, shaded by a striped umbrella, I found Clarence twisted, on his belly, crawling after the tails of pigeons that had gathered to peck at a discarded piece of cake. His felt hat with the mustard-colored feather had fallen off his head.

A fat man who was reading *Les Cahiers du Charlemagne* retrieved Clarence's hat, breathing heavily, and asked permission to sit with us. Subsequently he presented Clarence with a blue balloon. Clarence shook it. Once Ferdinand had given him a balloon with pebbles inside. (It was his first birthday party.) He had never forgotten it. Hearing nothing, he let it fly away. I apologized, fearing that the Frenchman's sensibilities would be hurt. But he laughed. His name was Pierre Zero. And he was professor of elementary plant structure at Hunter College. In addition to this he painted a little and wrote historical novels. They were usually about French kings or great generals.

Clarence stared at his beard which was a huge, unplucked bush the color of dull copper. And at his thick spectacles, almost as thick as his own. Simultaneously we fell in love with Pierre.

"I have crossed many oceans and dined with beggars and princes. But this is where I would rest," he said, placing his warm fleshy fingers over mine. Sometimes after a dinner of fried chicken and sherry he would become melancholy, watching Clarence and me with tears falling from his eyes.

"Everything sweet must vanish," he whispered, as I drank his tears.

He lay on the tweed carpet under lamplight, reading or scribbling dialogues for his novel. Clarence climbed over him, exploring his hairy ears and the soft flesh beneath his beard. I gave Clarence plates of shelled walnuts to feed to Pierre as he worked. Or I interrupted momentarily, to kiss his bald head or to tickle him where the rolls of fat covered his ribs.

"I am richer than all kings," he would say.

When the time ran out, he took his musical watch from his vest pocket. After listening to the chimes, he shook his head sadly. Sometimes he sighed as he wound the long hand-knitted scarf around his neck. (He wore it regardless of the weather.)

Each night the ritual was repeated. Clarence would take Pierre's soft hand and pull him into my bedroom, indicating the double bed. Sometimes he removed the spread and reached up to unwind Pierre's scarf. (Clarence can do things like that.)

We were both disappointed when Pierre shook his head, bowed and vanished into the dark night. We watched from the window as his huge figure moved slowly out of sight.

—

Every Sunday afternoon, Pierre Zero waited for us on the terrace of the Zoo Cafeteria. We usually arrived at two o'clock, after watering the tree. Our rolls and Jell-O were waiting, as well as a small surprise for Clarence. Pierre finally understood that Clarence liked fuzzy feathery things, or else things that made noise. This is because his eyes are not so good.

"My dear, you look charming," he would say, kissing my hand.

Later we prepared a huge dinner. Clarence and Pierre patted tiny French cakes filled with almonds and shredded coconut. I put these into the oven, and in a little while a sweet hot odor went all over the apartment. Pierre's face glistened with anticipation.

Occasionally we saw a late afternoon movie or visited the planetarium. If Clarence fell asleep, early, we made love on the sofa. Pierre did not like to go into the double bed.

These festive Sundays continued through the middle of August. Clarence was happy. And I had finally stopped taking the pills I had been given when I came out of the mental institution. I didn't think about that very much now.

I was in a great hurry to see Pierre one Sunday. Clarence had gotten something in his eye, and I couldn't get it out. We ran up the terrace steps to find Pierre, who was very good at getting dust out of Clarence's eyes. But he was not there. We waited all day underneath the green umbrella, forgetting to eat. The sun went down and Clarence began to cry. (It washed the dust from his eye.) Then it rained. I took his hand and we hurried across the park to the damp sidewalk steaming with fresh rain. Holding his face up to it, he laughed and patted his cheeks. We rode home in a taxi.

It was quite inside. Clarence did not play with his toys or eat anything. When I forced him, he vomited. I should not do that.

It was like that many weeks and many Sundays; waiting there all day and then Clarence vomiting. I didn't feel well either. And I lost my job selling hats in Gimbels department store. (I had done that after returning from the circus.)

I'm sorry that I ever called Hunter College because they never heard of a Professor Pierre Zero. He wasn't in any phone book either. I ran an ad in the paper, and then I gave up.

Things became flat, remote—but I didn't want to go back into the institution, so I took the pills again. There was Clarence to think about. And the magnolia tree to look after.

FERDINAND'S ROAD

The road that Ferdinand chose was long. He walked between burnt patches of grass. It was hot and no wind blew to cool the perspiration that dripped from his brow. He wiped his nose and forehead with a crushed red handkerchief he always carried.

The midgets, Sylvia and Honey, walked a distance in front of him, chattering in thin voices. A word or a laugh fell slowly toward him, but he didn't listen too carefully.

Occasionally he turned and looked over his shoulder, waiting until the lame elephant, Josephine, appeared with Clarence on her back. Clarence rested comfortably, his thin arms around the elephant's neck. Ferdinand smiled. He thought of the child's mother, who was still asleep in her trailer. Yesterday she had been in one of her nervous conditions; silent, staring beyond him, far away and trembling a little. He didn't understand but accepted it. When he held her in his arms, she had cried and then seemed better. He had watched her sleeping, and finally had gone to sleep himself. She had smiled at him before she fell asleep.

A few more days with the circus and she'd be changed, he thought. He began to hum as he thought of her smile, and how she would come down later to see his act. Then in the evening, he would ask her to marry him. A small cry behind him made him stop. Clarence had fallen off the elephant and lay on the ground, not moving. Honey and Sylvia had stopped chattering and were running backward.

His face was bluish, and saliva was coming out of his mouth. Ferdinand put a twig between Clarence's teeth and waited. Soon he woke up and ran into Ferdinand's arms. Sylvia and Honey kissed him and began walking and chattering again.

Ferdinand lifted Clarence onto his shoulders, and after whispering something to Josephine, continued toward the circus tent. The elephant followed obediently.

Seeing the huge Sunday crowd, Ferdinand's chest heaved with pride and excitement. He used to be a mute, tattooed man who merely displayed his body. But love had inspired him. Finally he had created a complete act. He joked with Honey and Sylvia, each sitting coquettishly on one knee, feigning fright or amusement at the crocodiles and insects that decorated his limbs. The crowd never tired of this trio. They clapped for more. Sylvia and Honey did a dance and sang a song; they rolled over and over tumbling and jumping. Sometimes, if persuaded, he juggled with them. Flying through the air they squealed with fright, but he always caught them.

—

The day Clarence fell off the elephant was the hottest, driest day of the summer. More lemonade and ices were sold than in any other year since 1928 when the temperature had reached 109 degrees.

Not a wind blew as she walked by his side without speaking, without glancing at him. Ferdinand wiped his neck with the soaking red handkerchief. He looked at her, wanting her to talk to him. But his thoughts did not stay with her; he was too excited. The crowd had cheered when he threw Sylvia into the air and caught her as he sent Honey spinning above. Both midgets had been dressed in gay fuchsia tights spangled with yellow half-moons. Honey had been a great success, singing in her high-pitched, pleasant voice about being in love with the tattooed man. Ferdinand smiled as he thought of this. He had written the song and all the dialogue, and he had many ideas he hadn't even tried. Cleo, the bareback rider had congratulated him. And other performers who had long tired of his tattoos wandered over to observe.

He felt annoyed that none of this could be communicated to *her*. She had waited for him, but she had not said a word about the act. "We've been asked to stay another week," he told her, hiding his gladness. "That's good," she said. (It was not the way he had dreamed it all those months begging her to travel with him...)

Behind them was Clarence's laughter; he was walking between Sylvia and Honey, who teased and tickled him. Shrill sounds came slowly through the dusty air. Ferdinand glanced back to see the three small forms drifting happily along. He took her hand, moved by Clarence's laughter. She had admitted two nights ago that Clarence had never been so happy; at least not since Carl died.

Ferdinand tried to pretend that she was happy too. But the week had gone. She had not laughed or taken any pleasure in the circus people as she had when she had been part of the pageant in New York.

He squeezed her hand, surprised that it was so cold. She still didn't speak. He decided to keep silent also; everything could wait for the evening.

He kissed her briefly when they reached her trailer. "I'm sorry, Ferdinand," she said, half-crying, and ran inside.

He stood outside for a while, not understanding.

THE SINGING WAITER'S SUICIDE NOTE TO ME WHICH WAS SENT ANONYMOUSLY YEARS LATER

Sunday Evening 1 A.M.

You—who lay dying in a mental institution. You—who may never return. You—who can take hold of nothing—are like me. But you are more patient with life. I hate you for it. I hate all docility. I hate you for being neither dead nor alive. I cannot be that way. I prefer to die.

I have seen and tasted everything. I have even loved. I have loved others. And I love you. But everyone has some condition. It is never enough. For you the condition was clear though unspoken. Only at the beginning of love is everything open. One is permitted to be free. But people *are* free. Why don't you learn that.

Like everyone who is half alive, you took everything from me. What did *you* give that was so extraordinary that you felt I had to give you more—to be with you, only you always; and our child. Yes, OUR child. Who else could have given you such a beautiful monstrosity that no one in the world can understand—even you can't, but you won't admit it—who but another like him. So tell him that his father was Joe Paliacco, and that Joe died.

Acting was important to me because I am no one. I never was.

I am only the people I can play or invent. And the truth is I'm not good enough. I cannot blame failure on bad luck. Don't feel sorry for me. There was nothing else to do, and I thought about it for a long time.

Joe Paliacco, your singing waiter.

FROM INSIDE MY TRAILER

I look out through the window of my trailer. There is nothing but dust—no green, no trees, no water. Only an expanse of land; bare, dry earth with rocks embedded in it. Where are the trees? The sun has set and the air is a little cooler. Now the dust is beginning to rise from the earth in small circular streams. If the wind blows hard, the dust will surround the trailer and I will not be able to see. That happened Wednesday. It frightened me, but not as much as the endless land I see.

I cannot measure things. There are no signs or familiar distances. I lose myself here. And Clarence; he doesn't mind the change. He moves gracefully here. He is part of the world of costumed clowns and freaks. He feels surrounded and secure. I would stay for him if I could. It would prevent things. But I am afraid. When people come toward me, striding hard on the dead earth, they have a grandeur and clarity I do not understand. Everyone is huge and separate. Why am I here? Sometimes I think there are no other people left on earth. The rest have disappeared or have been castrated. We remain, in whatever state, to continue man. Deformity is normal, particularly where no trees grow.

On the circus grounds everything changes again. There we are, the outcast performers and the spectators. Can I choose which I want to be, or has it already been decided? (Sometimes I wish I had a hump. It would be easier, I think.)

—

If I lift the shade on the other side I will see the light from Ferdinand's kitchen. It would not comfort me; he does not know me, and I do not understand the rhythm of his mind. I cannot speak to Ferdinand; we can only touch. Then there are no barriers. But I do not love him. I do not want to travel with the freaks. And I do not know how to go anywhere else. Clarence is so happy. He waits for the day. He rides the lame elephant and communicates with the midgets. No one cares that he shrieks or falls, or that he does not know where he is going.

IN FERDINAND'S TRAILER

Ferdinand sat on the cot inside his trailer. He read from the scriptures of Mary Baker Eddy. Then he prayed. He prayed that the woman might be happy and that she would stay with the circus. He prayed that she would grow strong. He did not pray for her love. Ferdinand did not ask that she love him.

Then he dressed carefully in a fresh green and white checked shirt with a small black tie and new work pants. And he shaved for the second time that day, until his face was smooth. He borrowed lotion from one of the acrobats and patted his cheeks. It felt cool and had a sweet smell. The last thing he did was to polish his old brown shoes. He had worn these sturdy shoes for ten years. But he hadn't polished them since the days when he had been a Presbyterian minister and had preached the Gospel. He had kept the shoe polish in the satin pocket of an old valise. He searched through his four valises before he found it. While he was slowly, gently polishing his shoes, it struck him again. He knelt on the floor clutching his stomach. He bit his lips against the pain and to keep from crying out. "It is an illusion. Pain is only illusion and lack of faith," he said, as it threatened to drown him. He groped for the scriptures and read ... Finally the spasm passed. But he felt weak and lay on his cot breathing deeply and evenly for a long time.

He awoke just in time; they had an appointment at eight. (He thought of the pain briefly and did not think of it again.)

Beneath his bed was a worn paper bag which had gathered dust. He knew exactly where it lay; he held it, thinking with pleasure of its contents. Then, opening it cautiously, he lifted out a small black box which he lay on his palm. Then he shook it close to his ear. Satisfied he opened a corner and looked inside. The emerald shone; her favorite jewel, set in a band of tiny diamonds.

He was the happiest man in the world. The ring would express all he did not know how to say. Nor had he purchased it hastily. Comparing, searching endlessly, he had found the most beautiful emerald in the world.

FROM INSIDE MY TRAILER (2)

Green is my favorite color; that is why I miss the trees. The grass where the circus performs is yellowed and dry. We may not be here much longer. But to what corner of the earth will we go after this? I did not know, or I would not have come. I did not understand the length of circus days, the monotony of the acts repeated again and again. Now I see it clearly with fear. I see it in the way Ferdinand walks, and in the slowness of his words. I cannot stand for time to move like this over such vast deserts. I cannot penetrate this world that is Ferdinand. His even sentences cutting through the dust fall dead upon me.

What miracle did I expect? To think of telling Ferdinand.

The only energy here is physical. Even the twisted and stunted hurry along the dusty road heedless of the weather. They tumble, careen, climb ropes, ride animals in circles. And I diminish. My body is weak from the heat and dust and sameness. I do not wish to walk or run or climb. Clarence is apart from me. Separated like a scissor snip, he is racing everywhere.

I do not understand the simplicity of their days. And I am repelled by the absence of mental energy. My own complexity spins against a flat wall.

(I have always been searching for words; not sounds or movements.)

Soon he will knock softly, come in smiling, not remembering

or else dismissing this afternoon. Yet I must be careful. The beginning of Clarence still angers me. I twist my fingers. Where was Ferdinand then?

If he asks me to marry him, I will scream, "Where were you then?"

EVENING

The diamonds had come to him from his dead mother's marriage ring. She had left it to him to give to his bride. He felt guilty about using the large diamond to make smaller ones for the setting. Emerald was unconventional, but it was her favorite stone.

"Clarence just fell asleep," she whispered as she let him into her trailer. Usually they visited other trailers, talked, and had a few drinks with the acrobats, leaving Clarence with Sylvia. But she hadn't enjoyed these evenings. He had hoped that the performers would like her, and she them, but it hadn't worked out that way. The entertainers had tried—telling old jokes and welcoming her into their circle. She did not respond. (They hardly remembered her as she had been in the other days, wildly laughing and swinging from the elephants' trunks.)

She smiled politely, of course, but the parties began to dim when she appeared. They sensed some reservation on her part, although they did not know what it consisted of.

Cleo had tried to win her confidence, had even told her a few things about Ferdinand and some trapeze artist who had fallen in love with a magician and left. "Ferdinand has been alone for many years. I'm glad he has you," she said with simple generosity. When there was no response, no confidence returned, Cleo felt hurt and angry. But she still tried to be helpful in any way she could.

At first Ferdinand had been depressed about the silence between his friends and the woman he intended to marry. "Give her time," Sylvia told him. And he used to think of these words often. Despite her nervousness and aloofness he still had the highest hopes.

This evening of the day that Clarence fell off the elephant, Ferdinand had asked that they be alone. She had understood and agreed. Yet there had been a reluctance as she bathed and dressed. She had put yellow bows in her hair and a bottle of wine on the table. But she felt confused. It was as though he had given her this part to play, this costume; and she had to play it through even if it was a lie.

And just this once, only once, she wanted no masks, no false creations. But how was it possible?

Suppose this was it, the role she wanted, and she didn't recognize it?

She felt a constriction in her throat, something she had felt before, and tried to stop her fingers from their senseless motion.

HONEY STANDING ON SYLVIA'S SHOULDERS LOOKING INTO THE TRAILER

They are whispering. Clarence is asleep, the dear. They are sitting facing each other at the table. There is a candle and a bottle of wine. She looks silly with little yellow bows. He is pulling out the cork, looking at her. He looks white or sick. She is not good for him. She's not good in the circus. He pulled the cork out and they are sipping. She won't look at him. She doesn't look pretty dressed up like that. He loves her. You can see it. She's looking up now. He is taking a black box out of his pocket. She looks scared. He is very pale. Now he is not whispering. I hear him. Clarence will wake up, the dear. He is saying, "Take this. Be my wife. Travel with the circus. We will be happy. I'll be Clarence's father." He didn't wake up. Clarence sleeps so soundly. The ring is green and it glitters. She looked at it and then hid her face in her hand. He's too good for her. He's pushing the ring into her hand, tearing her hand away from her face. She is crying. She'll wake up Clarence. It sparkles. She won't take it. He's saying he hoped it wouldn't be too late and that he could make it up to her. (I don't know what.) She looks ugly and she's shouting, "Why is it now, not then? Why is it now, not then?" He looks terrible and is holding his stomach with his eyes closed. But she doesn't notice. She's throwing her yellow bows on the floor stamping on them. "I want to go home," she is crying. I don't like her. He doesn't know what to do with the ring. First it's on the table. Then in his pocket without the black box. Now it's in the black box on the table.

She is getting up and standing with her head on his chest saying something I can't hear. She is kissing his cheek. He is patting her head. It makes me laugh. His eyes are funny. They look old. I never saw Ferdinand's eyes look like that. He is patting her on the shoulder and running out with the black box in his hand, not to his trailer, just somewhere.

She is still crying with her head on the table. She looks a mess. You probably feel sorry for her. I don't. I think she's stupid.

—

It was light when Ferdinand returned to his trailer. He did not have the black box. But he knew where he had buried it. If he ever needed it he knew where it was. No one would ever find it.

In his trailer he washed, shaved, and started off early for the circus grounds. He would not say good-by. He did not want to see her again, unless, of course, she changed her mind. He would help set up the tent and stands. He would write a new song. Later everyone would cheer. In the evening he would drink with the acrobats until he couldn't think. Then he would sleep. The make-up would hide the night; everything would shimmer and flow just as it always did.

She had not slept either but had packed instead. There was no point in staying another day. Sylvia and Honey had come to say good-by to Clarence. Other circus people hung around, not knocking at the door, but observing from a distance. Clarence did not know what was happening. He was waiting for Ferdinand, who usually brought his elephant in the morning. He ran back and forth in front of the trailer shrieking and falling. Something was wrong. But Honey and Sylvia calmed him down.

—

It would be a five-hour drive in one of the laborer's trucks and they would come to the train terminal.

CARL'S DREAM BEFORE HE DIES

It is so quiet. Clarence and I in a green glass box. We look outside. I am scared, but Clarence holds my hand. He holds it too tight. I talk. Clarence doesn't answer. He doesn't know how. He laughs and makes sounds. I like them. His mother is outside the green box with big flowers. She won't break it. There is no door. I am glad. But I am also afraid. Clarence is not afraid. He dances inside the box and falls. I fall too. It is pretty. Everything is green. My mother is green standing over me. "Please don't break it," I beg. She doesn't know what I mean. Her hand is on my head. "He is hot," I hear her say. She moves around slowly, big and green. "Talk, Clarence," I say. But he smiles. He won't talk. "I love you," I say kissing his neck. It gets all wet. My mother kisses me. "I love you too, Carl," she says. I can hardly see her any more. The green box is getting thick. I try to see through it. His mother's hands are close to the box. I think she is tapping, wanting him to come out. I know he will never go away. His father is not there. My father is not there. We have mothers. He has one. I have one. He doesn't have a father. I punch the glass box, wanting it to break and make sounds. Then we can dance around and shout. I am frightened. It gets harder and harder. My mother's voice is coming from far away. She isn't in our box. She is too big. I want Clarence to talk, because I am afraid. But he can't. He presses his cheek on the side of the green glass. He closes his eyes. "Wake up Clarence," I shout. The glass is getting too hot for me. I don't want to stay in the box any more. I want to run with him. I want him to wake up. "It won't be long now," says a voice I don't know. It is a man who is with mother. I wish they would go away so Clarence and I could break the glass. We would be careful. And not get cut. The man isn't my father. I don't have any. It is wet all over inside. Clarence and I are sweating, dripping water from our heads and bodies. I hope he will stay with me. He turns toward me and hugs me so hard it almost hurts. Then the box isn't green. It becomes darker and darker. I can see nothing, only feel that Clarence is hugging me.

PIERRE ZERO

Slowly he unwound his long woolen scarf, passing large squares of dark blue, smaller stripes of gray, and the chaotic insertions of white; white yellowed from secretions of his chubby neck, his thick fingers, the places it had been tossed, and time. He hated taking it off. And he wore it even in the spring. He took it with him into air-conditioned movie houses in the summer.

He sighed, pulling out his pocket watch which hung on a long chain. What did it matter? He replaced it immediately, and he sat in the old wicker chair with its dull rose cushion, stained and faded so the white flowers were barely visible. The wicker work creaked under his weight, giving him a moment of doubt. A bit of wetness came into his left hand. Then he closed his eyes and relaxed.

The hotel room was silent. And the shade, like old parchment, was pulled irrevocably down. He did not like to look at the night; at the blazing street lamps and sudden flaming car lights. Down, past the noise of Times Square, he had found this perfect hotel. Not far from the Hudson River, past noise and most life, it suited him. The sign which said TRANSIENTS was outside his window. It pleased him to know it was there. It pleased him that everything was dark, old, warm, and simple.

When Anne, his young wife, had gone away suddenly, unexpectedly, he had left their apartment with its dainty clutter, her yellow canary, and the false crystal plates and glasses she loved to buy. Abruptly, without a thought or plan, he had sought out this place, and he recognized it at once. Nor had he returned to the high school where he had taught English literature to gifted children. Without notice, he simply disappeared, changing his name to Pierre Zero. He grew a thick beard the color of dull copper and wore spectacles that he did not need. With his growing corpulence and disregard of the details of personal cleanliness, he would never be recognized. However, he avoided the streets where they used to walk, those surrounding the high school, and those where his former friends had lived.

—

Often he was taken for a scholar. Sitting at a table on the terrace in Central Park, he scratched meaningless dialogues in notebooks, conceived of novels that he never wrote and dreamed of great kings. Once he bought a set of water colors and tried to paint Anne's face. But he could not. Nothing else interested him, so he put the water colors aside.

After a year of celibacy, he began to have encounters—no one more than once. He could stand no one more than once. Drunk, he could imagine her delicate face, her young submissive eyes, and her lovely smile. Her young vacant smile had enchanted him from the beginning. The veiled eyes which saw little, which never probed or asked the meaning of things, had inspired him. Her fragile, tenuous joy fluttering about him had made him feel young and happy. (Twice he could not employ his vision; not with the same woman.)

The third year after Anne had deserted him, after his habits were definite, monotonous, predictable—that was the year he met Clarence and his mother. He thought of her often, but never romantically, nor did he attempt to superimpose Anne's image on her personality. He liked her and felt empathy with her detachment from others. He sensed that she had lost things, that life had taken and taken from her. And he liked Clarence, "the mad child," as he called him when he was alone in his hotel room. "The mad child," and "the woman" or "the mother." Those were their names. And that was the way he saw them. The woman was young but had no youth. He doubted that she had ever had one. In place of youth were eyes that were old with need. (This frightened Pierre. It attracted him and finally frightened him away.)

She listened to everything he said; her eyes never straying, never seeming to be bored. (Anne used to hum and smile, not hearing him. Or she had fingered her crystals, teased her bird.) He was content in this house with the child crawling all over him; squealing, delighted to see him.

Deliberately she hid her need, disappearing, trying not to stifle him, leaving him alone to read or wander about the apartment as he chose. But something oppressed him. After a time he had to leave. He longed for his dark room and his quiet. He became bored and restless. She tried to hide her disappointment when he announced his departure. She tried so hard.

He felt sorry for her and resolved to stay overnight. He planned it, carrying his toothbrush in an inner pocket and a change of socks. But he couldn't do it. It was simple. He didn't love the woman and never could.

"I am richer than all kings," he would say surrounded by her warmth, her solicitude. But he said it to be polite. And because he knew it was how he ought to feel, considering his three years of loneliness.

But he was used to sleeping alone, without really undressing; not brushing his teeth, taking off his shoes and socks, and loosening his belt. He liked to lie there staring at the cracked ceiling, drinking heavy purple wine, remembering Anne. No, he didn't love the woman. And he feared that in some way she was depending upon him. This made him increasingly uneasy. He had told her many lies, and then one had led to another. He did not wish to retract the things he had said about his life. And he had no wish to take care of her as he had wished to care for his Anne.

And one day he did not return. He had not the courage to tell them. Nor the inclination. He just went in the way that Anne had gone. That says everything, he thought. He stopped going to the terrace in Central Park forever. It was the only place that Clarence and the woman could ever find him.

THE ZOO

The zoo is our home. Between the entrances and exits of pain, crises—someone has deserted us, we are alone, the circus is far away—it provides a refuge. It is not always the same. Like us, it changes in small but important ways. For example, the elephants disappear. Are they diseased? Have they been sold? We do not try to find out. We feel the absence and walk on to something else. Next to the elephant's outdoor cage is the cage of the llama (Llama Glama, Habitat Peru and Africa). The llama is graceful, arrogant, still. We have no affinity with her. Perhaps we should try harder, since the elephants have been removed. "Llama Glama," I say to Clarence, but he looks at the sky. Birds are passing; ordinary sparrows or sea gulls. I have meant to find out so I can tell him. How high can pigeons fly, or ducks? With all our trips to the zoo we have not found this out. We tend to stare at parts of things; like stones. Hypnotized by the sun, the large seals stay out of the water for a long time turning copper or whitish brown. We do not go to the zoo to learn. I do not assimilate new things quickly. Nor am I very curious. We just look.

I spread newspapers on a bench when it has rained, as near as possible to the ducks. One duck likes to hold a leg beneath its wing. It is incomprehensible and interesting. I would like to wade out to the ducks' rock with Clarence, but we do not have boots that are high enough, and the water is scummy. Even the ducks have to shake and scratch their wet chests to get rid of the mosquitoes. Perhaps they are just fleas. He is stared at less in the zoo than anywhere else. I don't care. It is just a fact. Many of the people on the benches are old. They have had strokes and the rotation of their globes is limited, or else the eyes are fixed forever in one position. Some mouths are also fixed in a smile or peculiar grimace. Clarence is not afraid. He runs to everyone. He likes old people, and they are not surprised by him. Perhaps their senses are dulled so they cannot see him, or hear his un-formed sounds. Or else they are senile.

He has his seizures on the cool grass. Then I let him sleep there, covering him with a blanket I always carry. There are crowds and offers of help, police and ambulances. But I refuse. He is all right. It is true. Soon he will awake and we will go on. There are pink flowers everywhere, and small white ones. I fill his hands with them, and he joyfully throws them up into the trees. Or else, thinking about something, he lets them fall half-dead to the ground.

Recently he has taken a liking to the bears. We watch the big black bear who stands on hind legs and then bends to eat the sugar cubes Clarence has scattered everywhere; inside, outside the cage. I am fascinated by the white nails of the grizzly bear, which curve long and gracefully. (Ursus Horribilis, Habitat, North America.) They eat their meat, urinate, and copulate. We have dinner as the sun sets. Chimes ring on the hour and the sounds of animals eating or resting drift through the air.

There is nothing more to it. Sometimes we see something; a lame squirrel, a flock of pigeons, a new flower. On occasion chil-dren make fun of him. There is nothing to be done about that. It is essentially the same. A chill comes into the air at about 6:30, and I take out his red sweater and mustard-colored cap. It takes us a long time to finish our dinner. Soon there are only a few others on the terrace; young lovers whose initial interest in Clar-ence fades quickly, or old men reading newspapers. They are also homeless and have seen everything already. When our eyes meet, they smile, revealing compassion, rotten teeth, perfect false ones, or empty holes. It is a good place for them to finish their lives.

On occasion another mother will talk to me. Guilt or curiosity has prompted her. She is usually nervous. I am certain her husband is sleeping with a young girl. I answer briefly and politely while she and her child stare at Clarence. She smiles down at him. "Hello, dear," she says. I have heard it before. There is silence while she fumbles with something in her purse and then leaves. I do not like the glistening ring on her finger. I am glad when she has gone.

The zoo is our home, and I do not want it invaded by outsiders. (Dr. Hovenclock would be disappointed. "She too has her misfortune," he would say. But I know that. That has nothing to do with it.)

The madmen and madwomen are different. The zoo is their home also, and I do not mind. I know them; women with gray hair streaming down garishly made-up faces, muttering to themselves sweetly, or else cursing endlessly at imaginary companions. They are skinny and wear long flowered dresses and dirty stockings. Some are toothless and have bony fingers that move in bizarre, intricate patterns.

The madmen are younger. They sit staring at the clock or reading a Latin text. Once they were scholars or artists. Once they were idealists. Then the world changed, and different prose, simpler paintings became fashionable. Ideals died, and those who clung were lost. Each is different. We have seen the same men year after year sitting at these tables. There are happy madmen and those whom something torments. Some are in rags and others overly formal with conspicuous errors in taste. By their costume you can tell the year they departed. And they know us too, in their way.

A lady who wore only lilac used to bring large shopping bags full of crusts to feed the ducks. Delicately she would throw a few crumbs from tattered lilac gloves while whispering maternally to them. And when anyone came near, she moved away. She knelt sometimes, muddying her lilac skirts, and waved her arms at the birds. They understood and came closer. Despite her competitors, mostly small ladies in disheveled black dresses and thick stockings tossing hunks of bread with vigorous cries, the ducks preferred her. Perhaps they knew her.

Where else is there to go when our own walls and mirrors confound us, throwing back again and again our two voices and faces?

THE MASKS RETURN

I wouldn't let them go further than that. They wanted to continue the exploration of Clarence's skull cavity and his brain. "To decompress his skull is out of the question," I said. Nor would I let them inject dye to get a better picture of his brain tissue. "You cannot drill a hole in his skull," I said.

They sat on a platform above me, hands folded and nodding with disapproval. "I think you're making a mistake," said one, sighing. "The risks involved are very small indeed," said another. "A lumbar puncture is an everyday event."

"No," I said, aghast at their insistence and intimidated by their unanimous censure of me.

"The key to every single thing that is wrong with your son can be found in his brain. At least let us chart his sudden outbursts of laughter on the electroencephalograph. There is a type of seizure, rare indeed but documented, with laughter accompanying the paroxysm. How often does he have those reflex-laughter seizures?"

I wished I had not told them about my son. His lovely laughter was a paroxysm to them. His sudden dancing movements made them suspicious. His relaxations and fractional unconsciousness, they magnified into something with mysterious implications. It wounded me, this dehumanization of his gestures. Nor did I know if I wanted them erased or analyzed any further.

"We have gone on this long, come so far..."

"Did you hear my question?"

"No," I said, noticing that they looked at each other, nodding in agreement. They all spoke at once. "Do you have occasional lapses, moments when you do not know what is going on?" "No," I said, but they didn't believe me. "The hereditary aspect," I heard one whisper to another. "Just as I suspected."

"It might not be a bad idea for you to have an EEG also," said one with careful tact. "Hyperventilation and the photo-flicker components as well," they agreed.

—

"ARE YOU WEARING A MASK?" I asked one of the neurologists. Instantly I put my hand over my mouth. But he hadn't heard.

"What?" he asked.

I began to cry. They thought it was my despair about Clarence. But it was about myself. The remark had come out unwilled, like remarks I used to make when I was in the institution. (I had thought the masks were gone forever.) A handkerchief was handed to me from above, too carefully ironed and folded to use. I handed it back, looking through the corner of my eye at the masked man. I couldn't be sure. I wanted to touch his face.

"FUDGSICLES, FUDGSICLES..."

"Maybe we've talked enough today," said the head neurosurgeon. The others nodded in agreement. I left, after making an appointment for Clarence to have an EEG with hyperventilation and stroboscopic flickers.

But I kept seeing the neurologist's face with a mask; not made of plastic or rubber but of synthesized skin. Only his wife knows, I thought. His wife and I. But didn't I think that of Dr. Hovenclock in the institution, of the aides and visitors? Then I was cured. I am still cured, I repeated to myself. Frightened, I walked swiftly through the hospital tunnel, tiled, curving. Confident that if I continued I would reach the coffee shop behind Atran Laboratory. What if the masked man was in there drinking coffee? No, no, I said to myself. If you think of him they will take Clarence away. They will put you in the institution again. I tried to count backward by four as I walked...eighty-four...eighty...seventy-six...seventy-two...sixty-eight...sixty-four...it was too easy. I could think of his face at the same time.

A lady passed seated in a wheelchair, not old, but weighing almost nothing. She smiled. I noticed blue pockets beneath her eyes and that she seemed frozen, staring straight ahead. Tubes containing liquid food were inserted into her veins from the chair. Maybe I am that lady in the chair. I tried to imagine it. And she is me. Then it doesn't matter if he has a mask. Soon I will die, and all that concerns me is the chair and what is going into my veins. Not being able to chew or swallow they feed me most of the day hoping my insides will work sufficiently to assimilate something. Her lips carefully traced with red lipstick smiled as she was wheeled around the curving tile.

"Well, how are you today?" said the coffee-shop manager from his station, the cash register. "And where is the young man?" he asked with great joviality.

His face is not a mask, I noticed with relief. "He's home with my brother," I answered, breathing more easily. No one sensed that anything was happening. And *he* wasn't there. I ordered a Coke and a grilled cheese sandwich. I made no effort to hide the three green and brown Librium capsules I swallowed with my Coke. I closed my eyes and tried to think of other days, of things I liked, things I had. I thought of the flower box which had bloomed wildly despite neglect. I felt better. There might be other windows bursting with flowers some day. The masked man's image had receded. I left without eating the sandwich.

———

"You look tired," said my brother Elliot when I entered. I hesitated, almost telling him about the masked neurologist, but I decided to tell no one.

"Here, have some clam chowder." Elliot was proud of his

cooking which had improved through the years. I ate, not tasting it, remarking how good it was, and what a good cook he was. I thanked him for staying.

"Clarence was no trouble at all. He just played with the copper lamp all afternoon." I started. There was a time I would have smiled. "He fell asleep there, so I carried him into his bed. He's getting pretty heavy. The bulb burned out. Do you want me to get another one?" He looked at me with concern. (We have been brother and sister for so long.)

"I'm all right. They think that looking into lamps or into the sun is a way children have of inducing seizures." (He didn't understand. Elliot was never sick. But he lived in a world of soap operas on television, and he was puzzled about many things. He was normal, but nothing interested him. Even that wasn't true. He loved to cook and to watch television. He liked it when his wife came home from work and they sat quietly together. She didn't mind that the presents he bought her were purchased with her own money. He loved to buy her presents. And he rubbed her feet and made dinner. She never complained about his lack of ambition. This was a relief to him, because people had done that most of his life. Even I did before I was sick, before having Clarence. I was ambitious in school and wrote many poems: mostly about dead leaves, rocks, and stars. Elliot failed everything. But he wasn't retarded according to tests. He went to a psychiatrist for a while because my father thought it would help his ambition. But it didn't. The doctor was puzzled and said he couldn't do anything. He said that Elliot was happy and had little resentment, unless it was very disguised. And his retreat from society was not like usual cases. My father was angry, but he didn't look for another psychiatrist. Elliot never changed. Nor did he develop his intellect. He read popular novels and sat in the park. Then he stopped going to the park. He understood people in an instinctive way. He made few judgments. It never occurred to him.

"What's that about light bulbs?" he asked. I was sorry I mentioned it. Even the use of the electroencephalograph was hard to explain to him. He liked Clarence just the way he was.

"We used to think he just fell asleep turning it off and on, or that he was interested in its warmth. According to the neurologists, looking into the light causes something to happen in his brain, and he falls unconscious. Almost everything he does means something is wrong with his brain, and they want to measure his brain waves again."

I had tried to explain it patiently, and my voice was flat and strained. At the end I had begun to sob. The more I sobbed the more the masked man receded. "Cry," said Elliot patting my shoulder. He looked worried and puzzled. He touched my hand which had long since put down the soup spoon. "Eat something," he said. "Just a little." But I got up.

In his bed Clarence breathed with his mouth open. His book of elephants, mended hundreds of times, was on the floor. I picked it up and put it in his bookshelf. I watched, wanting to embrace him. I cried silently. But they don't know him. I remembered the days when he painted and when he played with Ferdinand on the rug.

It had been months since he had played with his toys or had done any finger paintings. I touched his forehead. I should have married Ferdinand. "I'm sorry, Clarence," I whispered. I hope you are dreaming about Josephine the elephant.

How they loved him there. And how different was their attitude from the attitudes of the diagnosticians and neurologists!

"Clarence, Clarence, we should have stayed and traveled with the circus."

THE WOMAN WHOSE FACE
WAS COVERED

She was everywhere; behind lamp posts, in the doorways of Salvation Army shops, pressed against the glass display of a movie theater—did it matter? We saw her from the window of a bus that took us up Broadway; we were not going anywhere. His nose against the glass, my forehead joined there too that day. Only her eyes were visible. The lower half of her face, including her nose, was wrapped in a red bandana. It wound around several times and was fastened in back with a large safety pin. Always the same, looking at nothing, going nowhere, she existed. I know she exists. It does not end. I do not know what is beneath the red scarf; whether her face has been chipped away, burnt, or simply miscolored purple or gray. Perhaps there is nothing wrong with her face.

When the bus passed, we did not see her any more. This seemed strange. It still does, although I do not know why. I cannot formulate the exact spaces between our meetings. But she was there, existing in the years before and after most things happened. I often wonder how long she will go on.

I choose that particular day because the bus stopped right in front of her. Something happened to me too. It wasn't the first time, nor was I surprised. I knew her already. Her toes came through faded blue sneakers, and an old dress, blue or black, I don't know or care, hung down to her ankles. Beside her lay a package covered with material sewn together from pieces of disconnected color and design; black with white moons, blue between orange flowers, checks, all old, frayed but firmly secluding her possessions. A bristly rope, tied and knotted with care, made a fair-sized bulk of no particular shape, but nearer square than any other.

It was raining that day, and her baggage became darker— oranges turned brown, blues black, on and on. She did not move to shelter herself from the rain but remained against the wet slate of the First National Bank. She could have stood under a protruding ledge of gray slate or run down into a nearby subway station. But she didn't. That fact aroused me in some way.

The tension in my arm increased. I thought I would plunge it through the fake glass window. I thought I would reach her with my hand. I cannot explain it, even to myself. Perhaps I only wanted to feel the rain. Clarence was very quiet. I think he saw her, but that could not be true according to the ophthalmologists. However, there has always been considerable disagreement. And I end by deciding. I think he saw her. I didn't try to break the glass or even tap it. No thought was formulated. I wish I had wanted to give her my transparent umbrella. I could have slipped back the window and thrown it to her. She would not have moved.

I have done terrible things. Clarence has always been there. The psychiatrists know. They have listened silently, not understanding any of it. Even writing things down, I have given them cards, drawn diagrams, and still they have not known what I was talking about. The thing I did to the woman with the red bandana was something they didn't ever care about. To me it was the most important thing. Or else they did not believe me. And they move too purposefully ever to see her themselves. If you have wandered everywhere watching pebbles in the pavement turn brown in the rain or send up bolts of metallic light, then one day, glancing up, you see her. It is the only way.

I knew she had remnants of a mouth because the bandana caved in at that point—not delineating anything, because it was thick and there were probably other things like gauze and bandages beneath—but showing a moving orifice. That was it. The motions of the bandana at this orifice greatly interested me. Yet I never heard anything, not for many years. Maybe I never did. Walking by, I thought it was a soundless wailing. I didn't stop to investigate. We were always walking quickly or riding, and usually she was across the street.

She was always standing. Yet that isn't quite true. One spring afternoon, a day when Fifth Avenue was mobbed with women in colorful suits and new leather shoes, she was sitting on the steps of St. Thomas Episcopal Church. Clarence and I used to rest in there sometimes. But on this day we were all dressed up and we were going some place. His shoes were new, and he kept bending over to touch them, not understanding, trying to understand the change. I think he liked how smooth they felt. I think he liked his new shoes. In fact he was totally preoccupied with his feet. There was no way to know if they pinched, so I stooped down, now and then, peering beneath his socks for signs of blisters. It was a happy day. Everyone seemed to be getting ready for something. Even we seemed that way. A few people saw her and moved away. They always move away from her. That is the beginning of what is so terrible about it. A policeman passed. They often did that; pretending she was not there. Maybe they knew something. Or else they were afraid. Her bony legs were showing above her sneakers, and her package (I do not like to call it a bundle) was resting on the step below. It was one of the many times that I had glimpsed the convoluted writhings of the cloth. "I wonder, Clarence, where she sleeps at night," I said as we passed. And then I went on to other topics as I have always done when Clarence and

I are walking. "Here is a bookstore. I will buy you a book. Look at the bear. Feel the pages," and so forth.

She was no beggar. I want to make that clear. Psychiatrists never saw the importance of that. But it was. She could have made things easy by holding a cup or an empty plate. If she had attached it to her arm or waist with a long string, so people did not have to get too close, they would have certainly dropped coins into it. It would not have been necessary to touch it or even to bend down too far if it was a wide tin bowl. But it isn't like her to do that. (And this is probably one of the reasons for not throwing my transparent umbrella at her.)

As a rule, she respected the wishes of the people and stayed in corners.

But once she forgot. I saw her in the center of a street, her eyes staring wildly and confusedly over the rim of her bandana. I am sure she got there by mistake. The men pulled their wives away and everyone left a great space around her. She understood. Clarence and I were in a taxi. We saw the whole thing. He rolled down the window. He knows how to do things like that, and put his hand out to feel the breeze.

I told the psychiatrist that I had considered getting out of the cab and asking her if she wanted to live with us. "We have an extra room, and you can wear your bandana and come and go as you please." At that time there were no men. It would happen for months at a time that we were alone and the house empty. He indicated that my time was up. And I didn't talk about her the next time because I didn't think about it. We discussed instead, the usual things—what my real feelings are about Clarence, and so on. Psychiatrists always assume that I have layers and layers of evil feelings about Clarence. I do not. I have done a terrible thing and they will not listen.

Because the woman appeared so infrequently, she never became important, not until later. There were so many other things. And Clarence was always needing medical attention. To be precise, we saw her about two or three times a year. And she was usually across the street.

Perhaps she was happier living the way she did than she would have been living with us. I felt upset about not telling the cab driver to stop. I should have at least asked her how she felt about it. The thought of her would vanish. There was the circus, social events, love affairs, and Clarence's development to push her away.

Only once did a psychiatrist ask, "What does that woman represent to you?" Those were his words. "Nothing," I answered. It was true. By nothing I meant that it was something too important to describe; that I myself did not know, could only suspect— and that after all in reality she meant nothing to me. The flaw with that is that sometimes someone who means nothing in reality can mean more than anything else in your life, if you or anyone else could find out about it. It becomes, at best, a partially deciphered code.

The morning of the day from which all else grows either backward or forward in time, was a silent summer morning. Clarence and I decided to water the magnolia tree, even though the petals had fallen off long ago. Still there were leaves. And it reminded us of Ferdinand. (We do not want to forget.) Then we sat on the terrace of the Zoo Cafeteria. We still liked it there. A year had passed. We knew that Pierre Zero would not return. We always looked, but we did not look very long. We ate our rolls and Jell-O and left the park. We wandered through the Metropolitan Museum. It was musty inside, and we had seen everything so many times. But he liked it, particularly the Egyptian tombs.

When the sun began to disappear, we walked to a Horn & Hardart in the fifties. She was leaning against the glass, staring more frantically than ever. And the cloth had worn deeper into the orifice. That worried me. If she wanted to hide something, she must be made aware that without precautions, time would wear away the disguise. But was it my place to tell her? Clarence. It was because of Clarence that it occurred. I was already inside the revolving door when I noticed that he had not followed. He used to like pushing it around and around. But he changes. It didn't interest him that day. She did. And when I came outside again, he was holding her hands. He was making sounds and she was making sounds; wailing, horrible noises from the enormous, cloth-filled hole. I stood there, uncertain. Sometimes things happen that we never expected. Are we to be blamed if we fail? Yes. Blame me. At least understand what I did.

As I listened to the sounds from this being whose wailing I had believed to be silent, as I watched her eyes fixed crazily upon my son, a self other than the one I understood came forth. She shrouded me. None of it is important. That is because in all the years and all the time it is microscopic. Why, then, have I chosen to magnify it by one million powers? I do not know. I must. The psychiatrists see it in context; a small event, a chance situation. And they view my action as very understandable. But I see it as the manifestation of the eternal doubt I have about every step I take, have ever taken, or will take. I am afraid.

After a second, a minute, I saw or rather heard that she was not wailing but laughing with primitive joy beneath her mask. Forgetful of the crowd which had begun to gather around, but not too close, she was animated. Perhaps it was the only time in her life that she did not stand or sit rigid and afraid, resigned to the ostracism of all humankind. She danced in a circle, holding his hands. Clarence danced and laughed, unafraid.

It was not their whispers that dismayed me as they stared, fascinated and horrified: "Leprosy?" "A cancer eating away her face." "Some horrible infection." "She's probably his mother, no wonder he's deformed; he's probably syphilitic also." No. I cannot excuse myself because of these remarks. It had begun on the bus that day when I was separated from her by false glass; my terrible impulse. I had pretended it was an impulse of kindness.

It was simple; too simple to waste the hours of doctors. But hadn't I wanted her to live with us? Hadn't I wanted to shelter her from the rain?

It would have been better if I had hit her or torn off her bandage exposing the decay. Anything would have been better than to interrupt the moment of her joy.

A strange voice spoke: "Get your filthy hands off my son this minute."

With a wail—and that time it sounded like the insane screech of a frightened animal—she looked at me with frantic wide eyes. Then she saw the people. She ran down the street making a high-pitched noise which seemed to come more from her nose than her mouth. She forgot her bundle.

I took Clarence home. If it could only happen again I would give her anything, even Clarence.

We don't see her any more. I know she exists somewhere, standing without a moment of happiness because there is no other Clarence in the world.

I don't really want to understand. Perhaps I could not go on if I did. Why go further? A part of me understands every bit of it.

A VISIT FROM SYLVIA

It surprised me when she came. I hadn't even said good-by to her when we left. Over a year had passed and the circus was in New York.

She wore a black and white checked suit cut to her size, a small straw hat with cherries on it, and flat red shoes with a bow in the center. I remember Sylvia telling me that it was too difficult to get shoes made to order so she bought them on the children's floor of Macy's. Hats were no problem, since her head was fairly large.

"I don't know what made me think Nick would be able to make me a pair of spikes," she said, laughing. "He just repairs shoes. He's trying anyhow..." She laughed nervously, the high lovely laugh I remembered, and extended her tiny hand to display the ample diamond of her engagement ring. "Congratulations, Sylvia," I said. I was worrying about Clarence. I had been bathing his sore back with alcohol, and he fainted or fell asleep. I wasn't sure.

"I won't be traveling with the circus any more, but Nick says that I can perform when it comes to New York." She giggled happily, lost in the green sofa, her feet just reaching the edge of the pillow. I put an ashtray on the pillow beside her and lit her cigarette. She puffed.

There was a silence then. I sensed something. But it was one of my bad days.

"Sylvia...I wrote to Ferdinand. He never answered. I know I behaved badly and hurt him. Is he still angry. Is he..."

Just then Clarence woke up. Seeing Sylvia, he laughed and ran on the sofa, jumping all over her, yelling, "Josephine, Josephine." Sylvia kissed his cheek and his head, silently noticed the bruised back, and hugged him. "Josephine is fine. She misses you, and she was sick after you went away. But she's fine now."

I am sure that Clarence understood. "He fell on his back," I explained. "Poor dear," said Sylvia, thinking of something else.

She opened her tiny red purse and took out the letter I had written to Ferdinand. "Honey took it, opened it and read it. Then she felt guilty about keeping it and gave it to me. She was always in love with Ferdinand."

(For a moment I thought of Honey being twirled into the air by Ferdinand, her sequins and spangles glittering as she fell into his strong arms.)

I was about to say something, but I saw that something was wrong with Sylvia. She started to cry. "He never got it. He died before that." Clarence, feeling the tension, was shrieking. I held him on my lap, trying to understand. I had always hoped. Then I began banging my head against the wall, not hard enough to disturb Clarence; just lightly back and forth. (He who could save us was dead.) And Sylvia handed me a lace handkerchief. This delicate gesture moved me. I began to sob and to rock back and forth as I held Clarence, who had become strangely silent.

"He wouldn't see a doctor," Sylvia explained. "Even before you came he had these spasms in his stomach. No one knew how much pain they gave him until near the end. Even then he wouldn't take anything. He wanted to perform."

"So I took away his last small happiness by refusing the ring and running away," I said.

"Don't feel that way. Ferdinand loved his work and had a happy life."

(And in his death more than when he was alive, I loved him.

The green ring I had refused became mine, more than if I held it in my hand.)

"We all miss him. He was a fine man," said Sylvia. And she left after apologizing for having upset me. I kissed her cheek and promised to come to her wedding. I knew I wouldn't.

——

"Clarence," I said, gently patting his back, "we could have stayed and made Ferdinand happy. Maybe he would have gotten better. Maybe we would have been better too. But nothing seemed wrong with him."

But Clarence only cried, calling "Josephine," the elephant whom he would never see again in all his life.

I tore up the letter that Sylvia had returned without reading it. I remembered, but only vaguely, what I had written.

I was sorry about everything. I bathed his back again and put him in bed.

"Clarence," I said, "why are things found out only when it's too late?"

PLAYING

Clarence and Carl were playing in the twilight. I watched their happy faces. Occasionally Clarence would forget and put all his weight on his withered leg. Then he fell. They both laughed as if it were a game. Carl's tongue hung out of his wet lips and saliva dripped down his chin and slid gleaming on his white neck. He said, "Clarence, run," pointing to the huge lamp post whose warmth had attracted tiny insane moths. They ran laughing and making noises of delight. And when they reached the post they put their arms around it, resting. Moths brushed their cheeks, but they did not mind. The seconds of hesitation were brief. Clarence, awakening, would glance toward the window where I sat, invisible. Or Carl ran suddenly to touch the newspaper stand, which was a closed green box. Then they would continue their dance as twilight became night.

The passing cars sounded like gentle waves on a damp beach. And when I reached outside beyond the flowers the air felt warm and moist. (The red flowers were blue, and the purple became black.) I too wanted the silent moths to brush my cheek. I leaned toward the light. The glow from the lamp post was as beautiful as the moon, and became more so as it grew darker. All life gravitated toward this warmth. Little girls whose roller skates had come loose stopped, bending into the light to fix them. And a man stood there alone, thinking of something.

For seconds Clarence and Carl were gone, chasing the barking of dogs around the corner. Hand in hand they bravely left what was familiar and then returned.

I was happy watching their play; I could smell the sea.

Gently, the rain fell. Not at once in a crash, but so quietly that they could stop and reach for it with their fingers as I did with mine. The drops grew larger, soaking the velvety petals and making dark shapes under the lamp. It was a warm and steady rain.

I did not want to call Clarence inside, but gradually it came down stronger. I saw the more frequent looks toward the newsstand and to where I was. But they didn't want to part.

Carl's mother came from somewhere carrying a small raincoat and a hat. I came across the street for Clarence, and reluctantly we went inside.

PHILADELPHIA

We traveled, Clarence and I. More and more often it became necessary to leave our apartment. These journeys were not long. Nor did we go far. But somehow they brought things back to normal. We had no other reasons for going. But we saw things. For example, we rented an apartment in Philadelphia the summer that Clarence was eight. And we walked those hot streets, searching, hand in hand. It wasn't like it used to be. It was something like marking time until the end. But that is not important. Philadelphia is a nice place to spend the summer. No one notices. And the trees in Rittenhouse Square Park are dark green and shade the benches. Sometimes we ate our lunch on those benches, watching people walking poodles, or gently touching the beetles on the back of the bench. They fell out of the tree, I guess. There was no particular reason to have chosen Philadelphia. And we never went to see historic monuments like the Liberty Bell or the Declaration of Independence. We just lived there, enjoying the small streets with brick houses. Clarence could touch the houses in Philadelphia, or play in Fitler Square. There was a large pink turtle made of stone that he liked to sleep on, and no one was ever there. There was also a stately museum, abandoned railroad tracks, and a wealth of gigantic sunflowers that grew there. We gathered these flowers nearly every afternoon. Clarence wore a purple cap to keep the sun off his head, and I wore a pink straw bonnet with a point on top that tied underneath my chin. I wish there had also been strawberries there. Or blueberries.

When the sun made us drowsy we went for sodas in an ice-cold drugstore on Spruce Street. In Philadelphia all the streets are named after trees. I used to recite them to Clarence. After the drugstore we went to Rittenhouse Park or to the art museum. There was not much in the furnished apartment we took for the summer. Our lives became patterned in this pleasant way until August. In August I met an architect and then an ice cream man who was also a painter. I met both of them sitting on a bench in Rittenhouse Park.

I resented the architect's intrusion at first. The summer had been long and peaceful. Clarence was happy, and I did not want to interrupt our scheme for fleeting whims, sterile promises, infatuations. It was too late for that. Too much had been lost.

But there was a muffled voice still alive inside me; it had been squashed too often to have any vibrancy or conviction; *I want*. Trampled by the years, dancing elephants, a tattooed man I had not understood, and by things I could not be sure of any more. *I want*. I had learned that somewhere with great difficulty. And it had faded. We had receded, Clarence and I; no one knew us or spoke to us, and we walked and slept at once.

———

The architect drove us everywhere. We went. Why? I cannot answer, since he never attracted me. Perhaps I thought he could save me from something. Perhaps I didn't care. He pointed out important sites and explained new architectural concepts. I looked where his finger pointed—eyes open, hearing, remembering nothing. I dreamed of the patch of sunflowers, of cool benches, and of the sudden ice-cold drugstore. Clarence slept. He did not like the motion or fumes of cars. Sometimes he shrieked until the car stopped. The architect showed no annoyance about Clarence. Nor did he pay any attention to him. Clarence was as invisible to his ice blue eyes as were the monuments to mine.

"The concept is spiral," he explained leading us into an unrented house that he had designed. "The staircase spiraling through the floors gives the feeling of space. The structure is only secondary; it transforms the space according to my will. I manipulate materials for this end. As you can see, I could only transform in a north to south direction. An African palm reaching upward and spreading toward the dome would restate the theme. Perhaps you wonder why the windows are tiny portholes above eye level? I am not interested in combining outer with inner space. I have rejected the concept of transecting planes altogether. I believe in an absolute inside space of which I am the sculptor. The portholes are for light and air—not to look outside the interior. There is enough play of space inside to interest the eye and to rest it at the same time."

He paused and watched my legs as I admired his work. I did not know or care. I was used to men speaking endlessly about their private obsessions. What did it matter? I looked everywhere, focusing on a brick, a ray of light piercing the porthole window.

My eyes wander uncomprehendingly over everything. He misunderstood and thought I was interested.

The next house had translucent floors. "I do not like to close off one floor from another. Although you cannot see precise forms you can see movement below or above you. It contrasts with the static material of the building." To illustrate, he ran up a flight. I watched his short, square form above me. He ran and jumped until I saw a blur of continuous movement. In this house the windows were at eye level but the glass was translucent like the ceilings and floor. "It provides visual texture rather than a way to look out of the spatial unit."

"I am married," he said as we got back into the car. He slowed up. "Do you want to get out now?" I wish it had mattered more. "My wife and daughter are at the shore. They love it. I go out there on Thursday nights and return late Sunday. That leaves us plenty of time." I was silent. It had happened before and meant nothing to me, only time.

"I think I can make you happy," he said. "At least I want to." He was sincere. I did not doubt it. He sent a pot of velvety purple flowers to our apartment. He bought me expensive lilac slips with matching brassiere and underpants.

Our apartment became a receptacle for hastily opened boxes, usually white, with pieces of tissue falling out, flying about the room in chaos. The potted plants never lived more than two days and I didn't water them. The sunflowers lasted longer, filling jars, Coke bottles, empty tin cans. And when they died, they were still beautiful.

The architect—I do not remember his name—meant everything to be fresh, beautiful, and uncomplicated. But how could it be? Neither of us was enthusiastic. He thought his deliberateness was eagerness and that my acquiescence was a simple willingness.

Each of his words was a repetition of words I had heard many times. The openness of his attitude, the care he took to make me understand the creative relationship he had achieved with his wife, the pride and interest he felt in his daughter. Did he think I expected him to run away from them? No, no. It was important not to stop for too long, even in sunflower patches, or on innocent benches. And I had dreams at that time that Clarence was falling backward as we walked. I would turn and he was gone.

We drove to remote suburbs where we tore apart the baked shells of lobsters while we gazed at fishing boats. His hand was upon mine as we watched the sun set. "Are you happy?" he would ask. That was important to him. "Very." I did not know anything about it. Drowned in the setting sun, in the ripples; that was all it was. Clarence was quiet, lulled by the movement of the boats. I did not know what he was feeling. I would turn to him suddenly, to make sure.

Afternoons were spent with shades drawn in the bedrooms of deserted houses; penthouse apartments overlooking Ritten-house Park, tiny pine-paneled rooms on Locust Street, stone ranch houses secluded by huge firs. He had the keys to a multi-tude of apartments and suburban dwellings. I went, undelighted, unashamed. (He often hired a woman to take care of Clarence for the afternoon. Or else he played in a secluded garden, or napped in another child's bed.) The Philadelphia heat, the long car rides exhausted him. I am sorry for that. It is one of the things I am sorry about. Not in exactly the same way that I am guilty about the masked woman. Yet it is something like that. I forgot him sometimes. And when I forget Clarence I forget myself. When I hurt Clarence I am also crippled. That is what Dr. Hov-enclock did not understand.

Where was Clarence while I was being loved with efficient exactitude by the architect, or tennis player, or mathematical ge-nius? What is the difference to me what their names are, or if they really exist? The crime, as I see it, is that sometimes I am not certain if he was in the house, in a different house, or whether in these ice-still moments he existed at all. (Clarence, do not go away.)

———

It was twisted slightly backward and very thin. Not that size or shape matter. It was the sadness that the sight evoked. It ex-pressed something about my life, particularly afterward when it lay twisted and shrunken. I wanted to cry. Not just for that. For things I cannot explain as much as I have tried.

He used it well, too well. It was like something that did not even belong to him. (It reminded me of my hands or of a pros-thetic hook.) He put it through such rigorous, tricky gymnastics.

In the end I could not go on. I could not bear the sight of it. Nor could I go to those air-conditioned bedrooms to applaud a performance which made me sense only more acutely the incongruity and hopelessness of our lives.

The architect did not object when I told him that I would not see him any more. He did not even ask why. He continued to send potted plants; purple or dark red velvety flowers. They arrived twice a week while we remained in the furnished apartment in Philadelphia. But he never called. Nor did I find him sitting on a bench in the park. I never saw him again.

Even now, the potted plants come anonymously to my apartment in New York. I water them and they make me happy.

After the agonizing afternoons and the directionless trips in the car, we should have left Philadelphia. I was tired. Clarence was no longer happy. He didn't want to pick sunflowers any more. And there was nothing to do. Yet I was attached to Philadelphia and lingered on the benches, waiting for something.

SEYMOUR

I put up with a lot. But that's how life is. I don't complain. I thought if I stayed around long enough, she would stop all the nonsense. I guess I'm a fool. There are others. But I got attached to her. She liked music and she needed someone to take care of her. I knew she wasn't crazy about me, but those things grow.

I was sick that spring when she made a fool of herself dressing up and parading in front of everyone. It embarrassed me. But I knew something was wrong. If I had thought she was really in love with that circus fellow I would have left, but I knew she didn't love anyone—except Clarence. She'd have been better off without him. Love is something that grows. You don't just leave someone because they are acting crazy. Maybe it's crazy to play the violin. Who am I to judge what is crazy? I didn't mind her writing the poems. I knew they were no good. But it kept her occupied.

It's funny, but I felt better when she entered the asylum. It explained things. I thought the doctor would make her see reason. But he didn't. Sometimes I wonder what they did for her. Not that the money bothers me. I never minded giving her money. They turned her against me, that's for sure.

Maybe I should have married her when she got pregnant. But I wasn't ready. And I didn't like the thought that she wasn't sure whose it was. When she was in the asylum I thought about the whole thing. I realized that even that, sleeping around with actors and circus people, was just a sickness and that she'd be straightened out.

I know I did the best I could. I don't express myself well. I'm just a violinist. But I have always been a generous man and I needed a wife.

I was disappointed when the doctor said that she would never change completely and that I shouldn't pressure her. When did I ever pressure her? I just wanted to plan a life for us.

Anyone knows that a child like Clarence should be put away somewhere. She could visit it and it would be treated kindly. The truth always made her angry. She didn't even like to admit it to herself. Those other men must have told her plenty of lies. And she probably believed them.

I saw other women. It gets lonely in Pittsburgh. Some were pretty and sweet. But I felt attached and I couldn't feel much about them. That's the way I am. I guess you get so mixed up in someone's life you don't stop to think of what's really in it for you. I was even ready to keep the child, since she wouldn't put it away.

Maybe they just couldn't help her there. Elliot told me that a year after she was released she went traveling with the circus. I was depressed, but I kept playing my violin, hoping that she would come to her senses. But even after she came back she wouldn't see me, and she sent back the money I gave Elliot.

She just goes on the same way. She takes the boy on trips, and they come back just the same. I don't interfere. I see her once in a while. But it doesn't mean anything. I'm tired. She looks tired too. I don't try to interfere with her life any more. It's better this way. I guess some people can't be cured, or they just don't know what's best for them. Maybe they realize it when it's too late. People change. I don't want to get married any more, even to her. I think, What do I need it for? I am getting better and better, and soon I'll audition for a good orchestra. I hate to play in the pit with the ballet.

She had something; she doesn't have it now. It was a feeling I got around her even when she was crazy. I felt alive. When I play, sometimes I feel something like it, but not when I go through the day. Things aren't that important. And I don't notice that many things. Other women, even beautiful and talented ones, don't have that thing either. I can't really explain it. If I'm in a restaurant, I just eat. But when I was with her, even if Clarence was there, it became special. Even the glasses on the table looked different. And I remembered it later. I miss that. Living can be a dead thing even when you are doing what you want.

It's over now. Even though I see her once in a while, it isn't the same. She's hard to talk to. When she disappears I keep track of where she is through Elliot. That's all. I'm not a dreamer. I know that it won't change. It made me tired. It's a tiredness you don't get over.

THE ICE CREAM MAN

"Ices of all colors," said the ice cream man, "green, blue, yellow, pink, violet, all the colors of the rainbow." The mothers objected. And I heard them whispering that the ice cream man was mad. But the children begged and were fascinated. He gave them enormous portions that leaned perilously from pleated paper cups.

He tinkled a silver bell, and Clarence followed him on his journey around Rittenhouse Park. He was there when the sun was highest and remained until the leafy trees had begun to cast shadows. He moved like a man of fifty and was missing his front teeth. But, as I found out later, he was only thirty-five.

"Do you have tangerine?" I asked him one afternoon. I hadn't expected it. Nor had I anticipated his look of despair. "I thought I had everything." And his head disappeared into the cold box where a rainbow of ices blended together. "It doesn't matter," I said. "We'll have two cups of purple ice." He scooped out the ices quickly and with great embarrassment and disappeared before I had a chance to pay.

The sun was setting and we were still in the park. I was wondering if it was time to leave Philadelphia. Clarence was still following the bell, so everything was all right. He had never regained his interest in picking sunflowers. It was something that was over, perhaps forever.

"Please come with me." The ice cream man was standing be-fore me, and beside him Clarence was holding the silver bell. He looked mad, with his sunken cheeks and the gaping holes in his mouth. I could not say no. Mad people do not frighten me at all. They are often gentle. I have learned this. I have learned the meanings of madness.

We followed him without speaking, holding the silver handles of his ice cart until we came to a silent street far from the park, far from our apartment. Up the narrow winding stairs he dragged his cart until we finally entered an attic studio. It was dark, but soon he lit dozens of candles.

"I do not like to paint with any illumination except candle-light," he said apologetically. It was a magnificent blaze of light. He had screened the windows, but the moths pounded against the mesh, insane, and infuriated. A few had managed and lay dead here and there on the floor or in the corners of old wicker chairs. (I have tried to understand moths.)

"Excuse me," he said, and disappeared into an adjoining room. The clatter of ice cubes was heard and then the softer sound of large pieces of ice being crushed with a metallic hook or instru-ment. Clarence moved toward the sound, but I held him back. We sat gazing through the firelight to his paintings; simple things—grapes, apples, pears—but rising and undulating like flames. Everything came to a point near the top of the canvas and then drifted away. Crushing ice, flaming fruit, I thought. I re-laxed in my wicker chair, protected, at home in what was strange, forgetful of time or inclination.

There were no clocks, no radio, no phonograph.

"Would you like to watch?" He appeared suddenly, eyes glow-ing and cheeks flushed. We followed. Tangerines lay everywhere; skins on the floor, pulps and pits discarded in wooden buckets. And in a huge pail was the chopped ice over which he poured the juice which boiled passionately with basil leaves and rose-mary. Clarence was transported as the hot liquid seeped into the ice, blending into it, throwing the scent of herbs and tangerine through the air.

"Have patience," he said, with some fear. Perhaps he thought I carried a watch or that I had somewhere to go. But he observed, to his delight, that we were willing captives. Soon the pail entered a huge refrigerator. Clarence began to cry seeing it disappear. But the iceman gave him the silver bell and carried him into the other room. He soon forgot.

It was not necessary to speak. "Candles and ice," he said, laughing. "This is my universe. Welcome."

I thought I understood, and smiled. Clarence danced with delight eating the tangerine ice that was taken from the refrigerator and put into pleated cups.

He asked nothing of us. "Stay," was all he said. And he escorted us into one of the small wooden rooms that he had built in his enormous attic. "You are very lovely," was all he said before he went to sleep in another room.

The days passed peacefully. In the morning we left for Rittenhouse Park. I waited beneath a leafy tree. Or else Clarence went, and I stayed home, staring at the paintings whose movements made me uneasy, or sewing his trousers or socks.

A week had passed, crushing strawberries into ices, talking in muted voices with an occasional strange laugh, before he touched me. His fingers moved swiftly, icy and steeped in something about to overflow. It was an electric quality; at once sensitive, at once apart. It continued like that; nights of magic, days of calm, he playing games with Clarence, freezing ice or painting chaotic grapes by candlelight. I wanted it to last forever despite the madness that erupted, while he slept, in ghastly sobbing, or feminine laughter.

"I love you, and want you and Clarence to stay with me… always," he pleaded.

"Yes," I said. That was all. We loved him too.

—

But things cannot remain. That is what I know. I have seen death. I have seen elephants grow old, unable to dance or throw their trunks into the air to catch flying peanuts. And most terrible of all, I have changed at hours, at odd moments.

I never asked him where he wandered late at night, or why it had changed. But just as he had let me keep my mysteries, my crimes, I could not question his.

It was only an accident that some desperate moth was scratching at the wires with such violence that I awoke. Usually I slept soundly, letting the candle burn to the end by itself; certain that he would return and unafraid.

The laughter startled me. It was the high laughter I often heard when he was asleep. And there was another voice I did not recognize. Slowly, I opened the door and saw them entwined. The other man was younger, and his muscular back rippled in the candlelight.

The next morning was the same. I sat under the leafy tree. And Clarence followed the bell. It was as though nothing had happened.

Embracing me that evening, he said, "It is part of my universe. I love you very much."

I knew we would be welcome forever to feed on the ice and the flame. But we had been greedy enough.

And when we went away, quietly, gently, he sobbed like a child.

POEM TO A DANCING ELEPHANT

(Written in the institution)

Forgive me:
I didn't know your dance was just a limp of pain
Nor did I mean to make you twirl on two hind legs
Until open cuts and bruises made you fall.

Forgive me:
Dream of that cold night
When like a monument you'll rest
A queen beneath the stars.

(Not I, nor man, nor flea disturb your sleep.)

Forgive me:
It is only a second of agony
Until marble-white your bones will gleam
Against black night
And soft leaves shield
Your glorious form-remote from man
Beyond the dawn.

MOTHS

The moths have always frightened me with their darting, end-less, incomprehensible movements ending in death. I have spared and killed them. And I have run away. Why, Clarence, are there moths?

There is something I do not understand. It pierces me in dreams like pieces of glass. The woman is behind me waving her arms, the red bandana choking her crying. I know it. But I do not turn or run. I only grasp Clarence's hand more tightly. Too ashamed to run, I walk quickly, faint with fear. I cannot stand the distance between the masked woman and myself. Nor do I un-derstand the meaning of it. What does it have to do with me that she exists on solitary corners mumbling muffled prayers? Let me forget. But I know that it would be worse; almost like forgetting Clarence, or myself.

—

They make a buzzing noise, hitting the hot light and bouncing away. I am sorry, yet I hide my head under the covers when they bend toward me.

—

In the dream the space between us never ends. And I wake up exhausted. It has gone on for many years. Sometimes I think that if I pick up a mirror suddenly, without thinking, I will see her face. Oh, help me. I forget and remember. She comes into my mind in the midst of simple things; when I am putting Clarence to sleep, or when a strange man begins to speak to me somewhere. I tremble slightly. (No one notices.) I light a cigarette and think of something else.

Clarence, does she appear in your dreams too? Do you dance and embrace each other? She is whispering something to you. What is it? Only tell me what she wants. Somehow I will deliver it.

The way it is now we are too close and too far apart. I want to touch you, if I could.

———

I do not like to see them inert, pasted to the lampshade or lying beneath it in the morning. How can it be avoided.

———

There is something wrong with it. I know it. Yet there is nothing I can do about it. We travel. Then we turn back. We go in and out different doors. Are we dismissed? Do we run away? That is not what is important. It is feeling all this now and then passing her tomorrow, looking at her as though she were a picture. That is close to it. And feeling nothing, not even a rapid heartbeat.

This is what makes me think of death, when having felt so much there is nothing. I would like to stay somewhere. I am surprised when I receive things sent by hands made of flesh, other hands. I am delighted when I receive velvety flowers from an architect who knows I am alive. Not that I understand it. There is no one to send violets to the masked woman. And sometimes in the night I want to see her so badly, but I don't know where she is.

(Ferdinand, did I create your death?)

My brother Elliot tries to understand. I don't tell anyone else. The psychiatrists have not understood or helped. And he says, "I will help you find her." He means that we will ride around the city in a taxi, since that is the only way he travels, staring out of the window. We will drive past all the places she has ever been. But where are they? No. He doesn't understand that it would do no good. Elliot would speak to her for me. "We can never find her that way," I tell him. Then he looks so perplexed and lost that I am sorry I mentioned it.

—

I have tried to understand the moths.

—

I think of sending her one thousand bandanas and a pair of new shoes. I think that Clarence belongs to her. But I stop in time. Foreseeing danger, I go on to something else. Is there another way to live? I buy Clarence a hat. He likes to try them on, making faces in front of the mirrors from Ferdinand. They line his room, sending back grotesque, cracked, abbreviated reflections.

—

I am tired, I think. I take a pill. We go away again. It is false. But I don't know what else to do. Haven't I tried everything?

Springs, winters, summers, beginning and ending. She is crumpled in the snow or lying on a bench in the heat, unable to move. I skip right by, holding Clarence's hand. Is it all right?

SYLVIA

It may seem funny to say this, but I always felt sorry for her. I've had my hard times, but I always knew where I belonged and what there was for me. I didn't feel sorry for myself either. After all, I'm not the only midget in the world. They're all over the place. I've got a good eye for them. And some of them are almost midgets, say about four feet five or something. It's worse for the people who are almost freaks. I'm not afraid of that word. My friend Honey always got mad when she heard it. It was harder for Honey because she was pretty and in good proportion. (My head is too big.) Men slept with her sometimes as a novelty, and she kidded herself about it. I always knew that no matter how pretty Honey was no normal man would ever want to walk down the street with her. Even Ferdinand, who was used to us, never thought of her that way.

When I first met Honey, she thought that some day she would leave the circus and live a normal life. That didn't happen. Then she tried to get one of the acrobats or clowns interested. But they just kidded with her and had a good time in bed with her. With Ferdinand it was different. Honey really loved him and was content to stay right where she was. She understood that the woman Ferdinand loved wasn't right for him. Anyone could see that. It made her vicious. But she was sweet to him when he was dying. I never saw her so sweet. After he died, she put on weight and lost her looks. No one likes her very much. But at least Honey understands what she is and what there is for her. It took her a long time.

It's a good thing that I was never a beauty. I liked Ferdinand too, but never that way. And I felt sorry for that woman. I think she was worse off than me even then. And now you can see that she doesn't know what she is doing or what there is for her.

I never knew what made her come traveling with the circus. She slept with Ferdinand, but you could see that she didn't love him. Maybe she knew that even though she isn't three feet or something she's a freak too. After all, a freak is only someone who is different and can't do things other people can do and can't go where they can go. The more I know people the more I think that each one is part freak deep inside.

So a nervous woman with a funny child and no husband is a freak as much as we are, Honey and me.

—

It isn't a great love affair that I'm having with this old shoemaker. But at least we can talk together. And I can cook and make him comfortable. He says he loves me, but I know it's just that he got used to having me around, telling me his thoughts. He's lonely. And I'm a little tired of circus life. I'm not so young any more and I think it's a good thing for me to do. Sometimes I think he confuses me with a child because of my size. But I don't expect the impossible. He calls me his "little, little one," and buys me a lot of pretty things. I've always wanted a pair of tall spikes. But my feet are very tiny and I can't buy any. He's trying to make me a pair but there's always something wrong with them. He's a good shoemaker, though.

—

I was going to tell her more things about Ferdinand, but when I saw her, I got scared. Something's wrong with her, and she doesn't take as much trouble with Clarence as she used to. I always loved Clarence, the dear.

Now there are things you never tell anyone. It might hurt them too much. For instance, she thinks Clarence can't talk. Well, he used to talk to me all the time. Not when Honey was there, or Ferdinand or anyone else. He would say things like, "Josephine the elephant is nice. She is my elephant." Then he laughed. Another time, when Ferdinand took her out to see the acrobats he said, "Ferdinand is my daddy and Sylvia is my mommy." He knew I was like him in a certain way. When she was around he just fussed and made noises. He could tell that something was all wrong with his mother. A midget has to see things up close. It changes things sometimes so it isn't true. Or else the other way. She should have left Clarence with us. But she was attached to him in a funny way. Even now, she wouldn't let anyone have him.

He looked greenish and funny and she had Band-Aids on her hands, so I felt sick and wanted to go away even though I hadn't told her everything. After she refused to marry Ferdinand, he collapsed. He didn't try to shoot himself or anything, but he didn't perform well, even though he thought he did. And he drank a lot. Ferdinand never drank before and it made his stomach trouble worse. (I heard a rumor once that Ferdinand was an alcoholic a long time ago. Of course I never believed it.)

She did kill him in a way, building up his hopes like that. But you can't accuse someone like that. She wasn't one of us and she wasn't one of them. I mean you have to decide what world you are in and keep to it. She couldn't make up her mind, and when she did, it was too late. That's why I feel sorry for her. She looks normal in size and shape, and she used to sound normal too, but inside it was always worse, much worse, than we are on the outside.

I forgot to tell her that he called her over and over again when he was dying. But why should she know about that? I told her the facts.

—

The shoemaker doesn't know that there is something wrong inside; my womb isn't developed, so I can't have children. But I think he's past the age when that would be important.

CHICAGO

We came to Chicago. It was like many things we did. Too many people were phoning, or someone died. Or else the earth dried up where we were. I can't remember what specific thing it was. I don't want to. After the circus it didn't matter where we went or why. Perhaps I was searching for another circus. Or I was looking for a father for Clarence. The truth is never clear, is it, Clarence?

It happens that we went to see a top neurosurgeon about the possibility of water on the brain. I remember now that we packed X-rays, and that a diagnostic chart containing all his graphs had been forwarded. It is so, and yet, thinking of Chicago, I cannot remember a neurologist.

After he came out of the hospital (yes, I let them cut through his scalp; let them remove something), we spent quiet afternoons near the lake. He did not walk or jump very much, and he wore a white patch over the incision. But he liked to tear out the grass with his teeth. The sun sparkled on the water, and children waved at everyone from gaily colored motorboats. There were many sails. Some were white. A few were orange or blue. (What had they done to him? I didn't know. He had fewer convulsions, but his left hand hung limply at his side, and they told us to exercise it. It had been fine before. How did I . . . oh, never will I let them cut into his scalp again!)

Chicago is full of grass; long green grass, and water. We threw a striped ball back and forth without joy. He didn't care. But he played with me out of habit. The limp arm moved up slowly and the ball bounced away. He found it.

(Oh, never will I do it again. I always say that.)

We were lonely for some reason. Usually we find things to do, particularly in a new city. But the hospital had made us weary. I thought of the circus, almost forgetting that I had murdered Ferdinand. Where was he? I dialed Seymour and then hung up. "His arm is not moving and we are sitting on the grass, dying. I made some mistake." But it was hard to think, with the incision still stinging and the arm not doing what it was supposed to do.

Everyone in Chicago is friendly, but they are occupied. They walk through the city streets in bathing suits because the beach is not far. But where? We couldn't find it. The salt might have helped.

I had a smile on my face, looking at the boats bobbing up and down. I know it because my face hurt and felt cracked from it. Clarence was perfectly silent. He lay with his cheek on the grass. His other hand was moving over it in circles. ("Oh, give me a home where the buffalo roam, where I see Doctor Hovenclod all day...")

At night we had sandwiches and Cokes in the hotel pharmacy. He liked that. He dropped his glass, splintering everywhere, making music. But the counter man understood. He never looked at us, just swept it up, whistling something sad. Afterward we sat in the hotel lobby. He stayed on the chair, moving his legs, opening and closing his mouth. No sound. I said nothing either.

In the hotel lobby there were some men smoking cigars and a few old women almost hidden in huge dark chairs. A man who trembled as though he were cold watched us silently every night. His skin was yellowish, and he wore a crew cut. He smoked and trembled. Sometimes he disappeared for a while. But he returned.

We almost stopped that summer. I saw it happening, but I couldn't help it. (That's the way it is about so many things and why I do some things I don't want to do and never intended doing.) For example, we didn't care to walk outside at night. And we didn't pick flowers or do anything. Clarence dozed quite often without warning, slumping down into his chair. He awoke confused. (I don't know what they did to him. He didn't shriek or have convulsions. He didn't laugh or jump or move his left arm.)

The man carried a heavy sweater which he put on when his teeth began to chatter. Once, when the temperature was ninety-four degrees, he wrapped it around himself. If Clarence had not been mutilated by the neurosurgeon he would have run, laughing and falling, toward the sound of the chattering teeth. Soon they would have made friends. But although he turned his head once in a while, he remained on the chair.

A silent communication developed between us. The man sat a little closer and nodded. I smiled back, my cheeks cracking. Clarence moved his arms. One stayed in the air while the other fell back into his lap.

Nothing else happened for a week, but we had a reason to sit in the hotel lobby. And so did he. Finally we said a few words; nothing witty or significant, just empty vehicles for beginning something. "Where are you from?" Things like that. And the exchange of newspapers and cigarettes.

He had been discharged from a veterans hospital and was not well enough to look for work or an apartment. He had no family and did not feel like looking up his friends. In fact, like us, he didn't feel like doing anything. He spoke with a smile that did not light up his eyes. His hand began to tremble of its own accord as he tried to bring the cigarette to his lips. (I understand about hands.) "Malaria and nervous exhaustion," he explained.

Did he have a prosthetic hook which he tried to hide, by draping his sweater over it? I cannot be sure. It is one of those details that is not clear. The thought frightens me. I would prefer useless cosmetic hands encased in soft gloves.

We were all dead, unable to continue. That was all it was. This moment in his time had coincided with ours. We left the hotel lobby at night; he with his false forearms and hand, Clarence with no voice and a hook or no hand (I am certain of nothing) and me with my hours and years going fast, with quiet explosions in my head.

Is it possible that my hand was holding a hook; that a hook was helping Clarence exercise his limp hand, that a hook paid for three tickets to a movie?

Real or false, he acquainted us with Chicago, which was his city. And Clarence's eyes became brighter. He found the beach we had been looking for, and we went wading.

There is not much more to it. We found an apartment and lived happily for several months. I decorated it comfortably in blues, greens, wicker and pine. Everything was fresh, crisp, and beginning. (The hook lay on the blue tablecloth.) Perhaps there was no need for it. We made love. But we never pretended it was anything that would keep us together. I would have stayed even so. It was enough to live comfortably and peacefully without the burglar bars.

But he returned to an executive position with IBM and became engaged to a girl who was young, lively, and sympathetic.

We were sorry to part. But it was all right. Chicago wasn't our home. And the arm was beginning to function almost normally, so I could conceive of continuing.

PLAYING

The hot sidewalks glistened with such heat that most children played beneath the sprays of nearby housing projects. If they were lucky, someone took them to the beach.

Most were taken from the burning asphalt and melting tar, and the streets were vacant until evening.

Clarence and Carl remained where they always played, to the left of the newsstand, which cast a small triangular shadow. Carl wore no shirt. His chest was white, silken, gleaming with the saliva drops that trickled from his mouth. His head was protected by a navy blue peaked cap which had a tendency to fall off. He replaced it himself, if he noticed its absence, or, with a sigh of annoyance, his watchful mother came from behind the newspapers to push it back with a brusque stroke. Clarence had a variety of caps to protect him from the sun; yellow, mustard, red, or green, depending upon the color of his bathing trunks. For that is what he wore on those hot days, short trunks with covered elastic bands to keep them around his waist.

These hot days were endless; but for Clarence and Carl they fled by unnoticed. I filled huge plastic basins with cold water and they splashed each other or soaked their feet.

One day, laughing at their new game, they placed their caps in a large basin. The blue from Carl's hat floated into the water and soon, to their amazement, Clarence's yellow cap was chartreuse. (They saw this happen, bending over and straining their weak eyes.) I glanced outside and saw Carl replacing his wet hat, un-aware of the blue dye that slid down his cheeks. Clarence left his hat floating in the water.

How I wish Carl's mother hadn't scolded, dumping the water furiously into the soft tar and wringing out Carl's cap with strong, angry hands. She left Clarence's hat in the empty basin, where it dried yellowish-green.

It went on all summer; the heat, the same pans of cold water. How happy it made me to see them playing with joy and absorp-tion.

"Water," said Carl, laughing and drooling when I delivered refilled pans. And Clarence jumped up and down squeezing Carl's hand too tightly until he yelled.

If Carl's mother cursed under her breath when she saw me bringing the water, she never openly protested. Let the water flow, I thought, as I lay in the hot apartment. Let them laugh, I thought, as I listened, smiling. Let it last.

It lasted forever, that summer of hot stone and feet pushing over basins gleefully. Sometimes in the depth of the water the toes played together; Carl's pearly white ones, all little, all even, and Clarence's bumpy twisted toes, darker and more frenzied in their motion. A summer is an eternal thing like water and laugh-ter.

And it is going on still, because I am refilling the pans that Carl's mother has angrily emptied into the street, or that Clar-ence has accidently turned over, not seeing where he was going.

They are, even now, wetting each other's cheeks, and then licking off the water. Or floating a variety of peeled sticks and colored papers that they have found and will always find. How can anything like that just stop?

Surely the fascination was not just in the water, but in the love and friendship that flowed between them. There is always more water, more and more and more.

THE MEN

Sometimes I know that everything is over. It is not because Clarence is weeping and nothing can ever be done. I hear him wailing and throwing things into the air and against the walls. It isn't just that; the disorganization of his play or the fact that he spends much of the time underneath the bed not wanting to see me. I accept that, since it can't be helped and is therefore no one's fault. No, it isn't that as much as the appearance of my hands. I've had the red blotches and scabs on them for a long time. In fact my medicine chest has always been full of ointments and salves to heal them. They did heal for a while. The red blotches appeared long ago; about a year after Clarence was born. I would notice their onset mostly in periods of silent contentment. A silent afternoon; the phone would not ring. (I must have been expecting someone.) But all the same I was happy bathing him, powdering his body, holding him in my arms. And then they would be covered. It was some sort of allergy and I was told not to eat tomatoes, or pineapple, or to keep away from cats. I believed it and followed instructions. But my hands had a life of their own. The red circular marks would begin at my fingertips and creep upward. There was no feeling attached to these blemishes. It was only a year later that the itching began. And after that there came to my hands a terrible combination of itching and burning. The dermatologists had more ointments and even pills that I swallowed to relieve these sensations. For the most part nothing helped—at least not very much—except the remedies I myself initiated. One was to scratch until they bled. The pain was well worth it. And after such a session there was often no recurrence for weeks. Of course some scars remained. But these did not seem important.

Now that he spends so much time under the bed I have much more time to think.

I am afraid I have made it sound worse than it is. He is not always under the bed. He comes out for the plates of food I place on the floor. Occasionally after a long nap things seem new to him. He tries on his collection of hats. (He will no longer do it when I am watching.) And once in a while he indicates by tugging at the door knob that he wants to go to the park. I always jump at this chance to be close to him the way we used to be. No matter how I feel, even if my hands are wrapped to the elbows in gauze as they are today, I manage to go to the park with him. I am delighted to watch him in the sandbox outside. I cry with joy when forgetting all but the second he runs over to me and embraces me.

Most of the time I am sitting with my hands bound in gauze, gazing beyond the burglar gates, thinking. It is strange that when my hands are thus bound I am able to think clearly. (Doctor Hovenclock should have bound my hands long ago.)

Men occupy my thoughts most of the time. With great difficulty I attempt to see them, to separate one from the other. For the most part they are bound together like a flat poster. But as I work at delivering them from this anonymity I discover that I can disentangle only the men who were already disguised. For example, Pierre Zero pounds in my brain quite clearly, although my affair with him was brief. I know that it is because he was a total imposter, a man with no life. He never told me that, but I sense it now. And therefore he is the most real. I can see the thick, untamed beard carrying soot, cake crumbs, and giving off the odor of slightly spoiled milk. If he walked into this room I would call, "Pierre Zero, imposter, fake man, liar, I know you. Come closer so I can breathe in your reality."

Even before Clarence was born I was attracted to masquerades and disguises.

———

I know too much now to consider talking to a psychiatrist. In fact if I had put Clarence under the bed a long time ago, I might have saved us. For example, I know that everything is because of silence. The painful constrictions in my throat only reaffirm my theory. I do not mean that I know anything about the origin of my silence or that it interests me. I am only interested in it as a clue to the puzzle I work on every day. Besides I told Dr. Hovenclock about it years ago. It was when I was seeing masks and vomiting out words, at least until a new structure was imposed upon me. "Psychotic" they called it, but also free. I said, "Dr. Hotcox, hands are mouths." He didn't pay much attention to it, being more interested in why I called him Dr. Hotcox. Or else he thought I was too disorganized at that point to make sense. I soon forgot it myself. I only remember it now. I think of it almost every day, changing the phrase a little. Now I might say, "For silent ones, hands are mouths," or, "Watch the hands of the speechless," or something to that effect.

And the men, returning to that subject again, a subject I cannot escape. Through their disguises I sought my voice. It is they who failed. I know that. Aren't my hands proof of that?

I have worked hard to understand my hands, even though nothing can be done about them. But I have made a compromise. Things have gotten no better with them. And when things change for the worse, so must the remedy be changed. It is no longer enough to make my hands bleed by scratching them. The itching and burning is so demanding, so commanding that I must catch it quickly. Sometimes I catch it in time. (Oh yes I fail almost as often, but nothing irrevocable has happened yet.) I once knew a painter who did his work by candlelight. That was not so long ago. I too have many candles that I light on such occasions. Thus I burn away the itching, or bring the burning to its proper culmination. No, I am not a masochist, and to the best of my ability I try to keep my fingers intact despite this treatment.

How peaceful it is later when, free of this torment, I soothe my charred hands with oil and wrap them in gauze. Once more I can think. I can see. And were it not too late, I could speak.

Yes, they are fragmented, and some of them, I suspect, are people I invented. But not all. Not Joe, the singing waiter, master of disguises. Joe could have given me a voice. He spoke with passion through the hearts of others. And he was those others— devils, jokers, kings. It was never conventional speech that I was seeking. It was a puppet through whom my real voice could sound. And he let this voice come through. Why, I could have been an actress and saved myself and my hands. I am no more certain of this than of anything, particularly since I chose to give birth to Clarence. Joe once said quite correctly, "Either put your two feet on the ground or get them off, but don't keep jumping back and forth." He was correct. I couldn't jump high enough. I kept glancing back. Unsuited to it as I was, without a voice, I wanted the usual things of the earth; that meant a baby and a husband.

Clarence often leaves the food I prepare for him, and I worry about it all the time. The men take him to doctors to find out what is wrong with his appetite.

If I have given the impression that I am always sitting here like this it is false. I see a variety of nameless male beings. I distinguish one from the other only by the most superficial criteria. One has come and gone from my life over and over again. He plays a violin. Seymour, I think, is his name. He likes to take us to dinner and to sleep in my bed. It makes neither of us happy. But I go. There is a hematologist with a moustache who talks about blood banks for leukemia caused by radiation. The others talk about different things. That is how I know who they are. But even so, I sometimes forget and only pretend that I remember. What is the difference. I do go on in my way. And Clarence gets enough nourishment to keep alive. What else is important? Besides, it may get better eventually.

One day, when my hands are better, I may find another circus and become a dancer in the pageants, or a rope climber. Or, as one of the men suggested recently, I might open a school for children "like Clarence." I didn't understand what he meant, but I can think about it, since I have so much time to think.

Sometimes I think it has gone on long enough, but who is to say? The candles are ready to be lit, and I am prepared for everything.

FERDINAND UNDER THE EARTH

_____

Being dead is not so different. It is like being a tree; tall, silent, stretching endlessly. Like a tree I have no heart or movement from place to place. A tree has desire, I think. But I have none. Some things went deep, and they go on forever. It would not be exact to call them thoughts. When you die you will understand that something can be there and not be a thought or a picture. _Have_ is the word I am looking for. Being dead, I don't act, think, or want, I _have_.

Nor do I control which things have gone deepest. In life I wouldn't have known. I have her, but not the way she seemed—sometimes half in another world, or sick. But as she was I have her. She is young, healthy, walking briskly down streets, her head high and her eyes shining. It must have been there. Not that the other things were fake.

The child is behind her as she walks. He can follow her because her dresses are bright yellow and orange. I have her smiling, laughing when the elephant stands on his hind legs or when the midgets are kissing Clarence.

I had the sense of sin. Now of course I don't. But in life I had it, particularly when I was a minister. Good was good. Bad was bad. I couldn't keep away from alcohol, so I felt the sense of evil in myself.

It changed when I joined the circus. I saw that things were created as they were; humped, twisted, cracked in the skull, twelve-fingered. Even seeing that, I didn't completely change. I pronounced my judgments, secretly, upon all humanity as I traveled east, west, north, south.

When I was away from her I judged her also. But the strange thing is that when I was near her I lost the sense of sin. She could do anything and it was all right; not that she really did bad things.

Sleeping with her there was no sense of wrong; even if she had beaten someone over the head I would have loved her. Then I was free.

That's how I have her; free of good and evil. I have her well, in exaltation, not in hospitals or unable to find someone to take care of her. I wish she had a mirror to see this. I gave them plenty of distorting mirrors from the freak houses for fun. I even sent her one when she was in the institution.

But this is one mirror I can never give. If I was alive it might make me sad. But being dead, everything is something you have. And there is no desire.

ELLIOT (2)

I don't know very much. It seems that things were better before, but sometimes people only imagine that they were. For example, my wife Sarah never seemed to mind that I didn't work. But she's getting tired of working in the drugstore. Her feet bother her. And there's nothing saved up. I haven't changed too much. I would be happy in the same way. I am even happy in spite of everything. I mean the way Sarah is. I told her I'll look for a job, and I mean it now. But she doesn't believe me. That makes me think it isn't so. But I would if she believed it. I always thought things were all right this way.

She looks at me sometimes like she is seeing me as a stranger. I say, "What's the matter, Sarah?" Then she just laughs or shakes her head. I don't really know what is the matter. Maybe we should have adopted a child, but she never said anything about it, and when I mentioned it she didn't like the idea. But maybe we should have done it.

She's changed. She won't visit my sister any more. And she doesn't invite her over. She used to like to talk to her. And she would buy things for Clarence. Now she says, "Elliot, you must be blind. Don't you see what's going on? I can't stand to even think about it."

I don't get angry very easily. But once I heard her on the telephone talking to someone about my sister. She said something that was a lie. I yelled at her. I shouldn't have yelled at her.

We just see things a little differently. Sarah thinks that people can be blamed for what they become. I never thought that. Or else she thinks that a psychiatrist can change someone. I never believed that either. I just hoped that something nice would happen to my sister.

I visit her, even though it makes Sarah mad. "Forget her," she says. I am surprised because Sarah was never like that. And how can I forget my own sister?

But Sarah isn't always that way; just on her bad days. She usually tries to be calm. "Elliot," she says, "you can't help. No one can, and there's no point going over there." I don't really understand. Sarah thinks I go to help something. But I don't. I just go to see my sister. I have never been as complicated as most people. Sarah is more intelligent and more complicated than I am. I like to see my sister.

She has these sore hands and can't really take care of Clarence because of them. So I bring over some groceries. I bathe Clarence like I used to when she was in the institution. And I talk to my sister. She doesn't talk much. But she is glad to see me. I know that or else I would never come.

Maybe Sarah is mad because I never helped her much and I go over and help my sister. But it's different. Clarence is under the bed and all dirty and skinny. He needs some soup and a bath. That is what I do. I bring some toys for him even though he isn't so interested in them. But he does sit on my lap. We always got along pretty well.

Sarah thinks she should be put back in the institution. But I don't see the point of it, particularly now. Some things have to be left in peace. I don't believe in tampering with too much. Sometimes I think that's what causes all these troubles. For instance, I don't even know if it was the best thing for her to have ever gone to the institution. I don't even know if she should have had Clarence. But there's no point in thinking like that. That's how people get depressed.

I did say once, "Would you like us to keep Clarence awhile to give you a rest?" I knew it was wrong to say, especially now. But I thought maybe Sarah was right. (Now she wouldn't even take him. But then she would.)

When I said it she looked at me with such a hurt look. I can't even explain it. It was as though I had killed her. She didn't move. And she wouldn't listen to anything I said that night. I told her I was sorry, but I saw that she just wanted to forget it. She forgave me soon. We understand each other, being brother and sister for so long. Sometimes it's best to say nothing. People talk too much anyhow. I have always thought they did.

I wish Sarah understood that it isn't that I'm blind or stupid. It's something else. But then I would have to say things and I won't say them.

So maybe I'm wrong about everything. But she's my sister.

A LETTER TO FERDINAND
WHICH HE NEVER RECEIVED

————————

Dear Ferdinand,

It has been six months since we left the circus and came back to New York. I am writing to tell you something I hope you will be happy about. If you are not, I will understand. I can't really explain why it was so hard for me. I had to go away. But now I know that out of fear I acted against my true feelings. At last I am certain of something. Next year I want to join you, become your wife, and travel with the circus. Is it too late? You have been patient with me for so long without really understanding. I wonder if I can ask this of you one last time.

Please, Ferdinand, we are not happy. Clarence misses Josephine. He misses Honey and Sylvia and you. I miss you. I have made up my mind this time without any persuasion.

Ferdinand, there are things I have kept from everyone. I want to tell you about them. I am hoping you will help me and love me in spite of them.

Help me to understand you, Ferdinand. And I will help you to understand the things that frighten me. Let me become part of the circus again the way I was in New York. I don't want to be just a spectator. I can be trained. Let Clarence have an act with Josephine. She is tame and will never hurt him.

I am sorry I acted so bitterly. Sometimes all the things inside me become confused and I act in a crazy selfish way. Clarence loves you, and you will be the best father he can have.

I would like to tell you I love you. I cannot. Not just yet. I think that some day I will be able to say it and understand it. Meanwhile let my desire which is from my heart be enough. We need you and want you. I trust you more than anyone in the world.

Help us to adjust to circus life. Perhaps we can begin with a place a little less desolate. I was not used to the dry heat. I prefer a place with trees and rain.

Sometimes I am afraid, Ferdinand, that the moment has passed forever when you offered me the lovely and precious ring.

Let a miracle happen. I made a mistake. Offer me the ring again if you possibly can. I desire this above everything.

ANY MAN (2)

I am any man. And whom I love I do not know. What I think I think when I do my work. Otherwise I do not think. Life is short. Anyone knows that. To take what you can is sanity. I am not young or old. I am honest about financial matters and do not cheat on my income tax. Whether or not I am married is my own affair, and what I choose to do in my spare hours is also no one else's business.

I am any man. I have my peculiarities. For example, I like lobster tails. I like them with a passion. I take my pleasures moderately. I am not too thin or too fat. And I seldom get sick. I take good care of my body. Nor do I neglect my mind. I am interested in the contemporary world, in social change and politics. I am curious about art, although I have never enjoyed it. I enjoy spectator sports.

I am average in many ways and yet I am unusual. Most women please me. I demand very little from them. I go in and out of situations quite easily. And what I have seen and experienced I tell no one.

One of the women I see is crazy. But it interests me. She does nothing all day except sit by the window and think. Sometimes I do not see her for a month because the phone is off the hook. When I speak to her, she answers in a dead voice. I don't know if she remembers me. Her child is also sick and demented. He sleeps most of the time and never talks or laughs. She talks very little. She listens to everything I say. Then she forgets it. Sometimes she forgets that we have an appointment and someone else is there. I am polite about it. I have a feeling she does not know exactly what she is doing. I am pretty sure that she sleeps with anyone. It interests me. If I gave other men her phone number she would probably sleep with them too. But I like to keep my affairs private. There is no one you can really trust.

I am any man. I know it is best not to become too involved, particularly with sick people. I have only one life to live. I intend to stay healthy and take no foolish risks.

It is not necessary to bring her anything. I know she doesn't care. But I bring her something each time. I bring her flowers or perfume.

More goes on in that house than meets the eye. But I close my eyes. It is none of my business. She is civil and polite to me even though she is crazy and a bit of a whore. I don't doubt that she takes money for it sometimes. I never offer money because she has a certain dignity about her.

She keeps herself clean and is responsive in bed. Just the same I wear something. I never take the chance of infection.

As I said, most women please me and with her there are no complications. There could be if I created them. For instance, I might worry about her, or the child, who looks half dead already. But why worry myself over strangers? What good would it do anyone? I mind my own business.

I am any man. I enjoy the good things of life. I make a decent living without killing myself. And I take several vacations a year. I do what is best for me, which is what any sane man does.

TO HAVE WAITED

———————

To have waited until now; that was a mistake. I know it. But I tried everything, even drew diagrams that no one could decipher—they were too sleepy, or too intent on something else. I mean the psychiatrists. I mean the men (nameless all of them), who were always preoccupied with something else. "Is it possible that you have gone on with me this long, so far and not understood what I have tried to say?" I thought of that often, meaning all those men who brought me gladiolas, meaning my brother or you. "Do you expect me to tell you the truth?" I said that to a psychiatrist once. I have always hoped for another way—that you would guess. But I wasn't thinking clearly, or I would have known that it was impossible.

Did you think, as some do, that an institution solves everything? That if you can walk on the streets again something has changed? I could laugh. But I never laugh. The fragments are all true. I nursed him, traveled with him. There were moments of great peace, such as the time we picked sunflowers near the railway tracks in Philadelphia. It is no lie that I held his hand and kissed his blue lips when he was having a convulsion. But what does it matter now? Oh, in a sense we go on endlessly. But only in a sense. Who is fit to decide? Who can be the judge here?

You may understand when I say that it became worse when we left the circus and returned to New York. And that I planned to tell Ferdinand all about it. I knew who I could tell if it became necessary. If he had lived it might be different now.

My brother Elliot visits me. Sarah only sends her regards. I think she is more embarrassed than anything else. I understand.

And Seymour, fat, simple Seymour, still sees me because it makes no difference to him. In a way, that is what I hate about him. He knew about it a long time ago. It was one of those unexpected visits he used to pay, breathing heavily, sweat pouring from his armpits, jumping all over me ... I happened to be bathing Clarence.

"Wait in the living room, Seymour," I called, but he wandered in anyhow. There was no lock on the bathroom door.

Seeing the welts on Clarence's back, he only looked at me. He understood. "Let me finish bathing him." I let him, pretending nothing had been seen. And soon Clarence was dressed as handsomely as ever in red corduroy overalls and a yellow shirt, if I remember correctly. Seymour never held it against me, what he knew. But then Seymour never fully accepted Clarence as a person. I did. You cannot accuse me of ever thinking of him as anything less. As for the welts, it was one of those occurrences. And why did it surprise everyone? Didn't I take him to every specialist to help him? Judge by Clarence himself. He always ran to me, even afterward. And I bathed the open sores with an antiseptic. They missed the whole picture.

Doctor Hovenclock never knew or guessed. That disappointed me. I had wanted him to. He believed in my love for Clarence. I thank him for that. Would he have still believed in it if he knew? Ferdinand died thinking I was a saint. Better so. But I couldn't help it. It was a feeling in my hands; nowhere else. Everyone has always thought quite correctly that I am a very gentle woman. And that is what I want to be.

There are exceptions, of course. But what is a flaw here and there?

Does it matter that I struck the woman with the bandana on her head with my transparent umbrella the day she danced with Clarence? Later I struck him also. I left that out because it means nothing. Who hasn't been hit on the head with an umbrella at one time or another? It all changes. I told you that before. And if a little change is going to become great, how can anyone know? I am all the things I have tried to be.

Clarence does not live here any more. So I go through the motions of living, hoping that he will return some day. I don't know who told the social workers. I'll never know that. Someone misunderstood. He was happy here, sitting against the burglar bars at sunset and going over the felt letters of the alphabet.

I worry all the time. Who will understand him? What will become of him? And why didn't I tell someone the truth a long time ago? But I didn't know or understand it myself. Whose fault is that.

I did all I could. Did the others, Clarence? Or am I lying.

And why do you think we went to museums and to the zoo, and were so rarely at home? And why did we have burglar bars on every window? I was afraid.

EPILOGUE

Play, Clarence, play; it is spring and everything has come out of hiding. Too fast the trees are leafed, and soon their dark green will be black and heavy. But look, come to the window. Even Carl's mother is humming as she cuts the rope that binds the newspapers. And an old man is selling bunches of roses on the corner. He smiles to himself, half-seeing things, liking to be alive but not expecting a golden blessing from this earth. Watch him. Let's be like the old man who likes to give flowers to young girls. He turns his face to the sun. It is new and warm. He needs no one; just the earth and the sun.

Clarence, play. Carl is waiting. See how he sits on a wooden box, his sweet mouth open, his weak eyes fixed on our door. He is waiting for you. If you do not go out, his spring will disappear. You, Clarence, are Carl's spring. And you are my spring too. I will watch your happiness when you run across the street to meet him. I will share in it here, listening to the flies buzzing in and out, dusting the window sill, washing the clothes you wore yesterday. Forget yesterday. Today blooms fiercely and for the last time. It cannot last. I wish you could greet Carl every day forever. But even that must disappear sometime. Hurry up. Finish your breakfast. There is never time to waste when the world is singing for you. Look, Carl is crying. And his mother is wiping his nose. He does not understand that you are only late and that you will be there soon. How can he know? Call to him from the window.

He smiles and his tears stop. Even his mother is not angry today. She waves good morning to us. Later, she will change, thinking dark thoughts and making herself weary. Her heart is old. That is why she will never kiss you. She is a huge tree without roots who mysteriously puts out a leaf now and then, without nourishment. Carl is young and full of love and desire for the world. Here is a bunch of flowers to bring him. He will smell them and chew them. There are no contradictions in *his* feeble mind.

ABOUT THE AUTHOR

ELAINE KRAF (1936–2013) was a writer and painter. She was the author of four published works of fiction: *I Am Clarence* (1969), *The House of Madelaine* (1971), *Find Him!* (1977), and *The Princess of 72nd Street* (1979)—as well as several unpublished novels, plays, and poetry collections. She was the recipient of two National Endowment for the Arts awards, a 1971 fellowship at the Bread Loaf Writers' Conference, and a 1977 residency at Yaddo. She was born and lived in New York City.

ABOUT THE TYPE

The principal text of this Modern Library edition was set in a digitized version of Janson, a typeface that dates from about 1690 and was cut by Nicholas Kis (1650–1702), a Hungarian working in Amsterdam. The original matrices have survived and are held by the Stempel foundry in Germany. Hermann Zapf (1918–2015) redesigned some of the weights and sizes for Stempel, basing his revisions on the original design.